The Secrets
of Barneveld Calvary

Also by the author
In the Silence There Are Ghosts: A Novel

The Secrets of
Barneveld Calvary

James Calvin Schaap

Baker Books
A Division of Baker Book House Co
Grand Rapids, Michigan 49516

© 1997 by James Calvin Schaap

Published by Baker Books
a division of Baker Book House Company
P.O. Box 6287, Grand Rapids, MI 49516-6287

Printed in the United States of America

Library of Congress Cataloging-in-Publication Data

Schaap, James C., 1948–
    The secrets of Barneveld Calvary / James Calvin
Schaap.
      p. cm.
    ISBN 0-8010-5755-8 (pbk.)
      1. Christian life—United States—Fiction. 2. Christian fiction, American. 3. Barneveld Calvary. I. Title.
PS3569.C33S43 1997
813'.54—dc21   96-37305

Although this book contains material from the world in which we live, it is a work of fiction.

Contents

Prologue
Joys and Concerns

For a few minutes almost every Sunday at the churches I've served in the last twenty years, I have left the pulpit and walked into the congregation to allow the people to express their joys and concerns before our prayer together. In all those country churches, it wasn't easy to get worshipers to tell each other their happiness and their heartaches. In small churches people can't hide, and they know each other too well to act. But many of them eventually warmed to the idea and began to be proud of the fact that at their church the great lid of the old ways, sometimes heavy and dour, opened for just a few minutes in every service and allowed them a bit of a different voice.

Normally, what the people announced were weddings, births, deaths, and assorted maladies. Occasionally, something approaching a testimony would be heard, especially if the story concluded with clear and sufficient answers to prayer. In all those churches, there were times my sermons—no matter how diligently I'd prepared—could never be as memorable as the stories they told each other during joys and concerns.

In worship as in life, however, any innovation eventually begins to show its vulnerability. Over time, week after week, a pattern emerged—often the same speakers rose, as much in an effort to secure prayer as to prompt the others to contribute as willingly. Even though at times it became, like so much else, somewhat tedious, I never stopped the practice because its benefits always outweighed its shortcomings. Many people appreciated the openness and the sharing, and wherever I preached, the practice became a ritual by which the people defined themselves as a congregation.

But so many times in those years, I wanted to tell other stories—more than birth announcements or vigils at the deathbeds of loving relatives, as beautiful and touching as those stories could be. Weeks passed, months rolled by, and I'd stand at the front of those churches with other joys and concerns, other stories begging to be told, stories I'd revisit in the eyes of the men and women and kids in the pews, stories I knew too well, but stories that were, just as those recited publicly, and often more so, *real* joys and concerns.

I would like to simply tell the truth as I've seen it, not something precast to win friends and bring in seekers. I want to tell you the stories I can't forget for reasons—well, for reasons which I believe go to the heart of who we are as creatures of God. Some of these stories I know from the inside, word by word transcriptions from the heart of those who were there. Some I know secondhand, from those who may have had reasons to put their own spin on what happened, but whose witness carried what I believed to be the heft of truth. And some I've had to build myself from what I know well of the people, the places, and the milieu of life in churches I've served on the broad plains of the rural Midwest, a place European explorers almost two centuries ago called "the great American desert." Sometimes you'll have to trust my perceptions, my versions of these stories—which is to say you'll have to trust my heart. I know that in this day and age, trusting the teller is itself no small leap of faith.

So these are the untold joys and concerns of a church I'll call Barneveld Calvary, stories I won't forget, because I'm convinced they live somewhere inside all of us.

I want to share them now.

The Profession of Crystal te Lindert

Even in mixed company, I've heard men around Barneveld say that a woman is never more beautiful than when she's pregnant. Older men can say that. Younger men know better, although they might admit it themselves if there are no women around.

The council at Barneveld Calvary Church is, was, and perhaps forever shall be exclusively male, and that's where I heard the line last, actually. It was said of Crystal te Lindert, who came to the council a few months back to make profession of her faith. The men around that long mahogany table took one look at the young woman who'd given her father so much grief, noted the healthy blush on her full cheeks, the new softer lines around a chin that had always seemed sharp and held about a notch too high, even snuck a peek at the new maternal heft beneath her denim jumper, then heard the woman's profession, and decided their fathers weren't wrong about women and beauty and being with child.

She'd come to them on her knees—not literally, of course. But she'd come to profess her faith in Jesus Christ, to gain admission to the sacraments, to join the church, to signal the fact that she'd turned her life around—or that Christ had. She'd come to assure them that she recognized both the sin in her soul and the saving work of Jesus Christ in her life. At Barneveld Calvary, the men in the council room keep the keys to the sacraments she'd come to ask for.

There was a day when the august group of church fathers struck fear into the heart of anyone who'd visit, man or woman, but Barneveld Calvary, like many churches, has lost the power to make those who come before the elders quake and shiver. Today, professions of faith are pretty much pro forma—no one has ever been turned down, even though I've heard almost heretical definitions of the Holy Spirit and seen commitment so mercilessly flat it would have registered death on a cardiac unit. I remember a kid I'll call Freddy who sat like a muskrat the whole time the council spoke to him, grunting only when the silence dragged on too long even for him. He still passed muster. Later, I discovered his brother-in-law had bribed him to make profession of faith with a loan on a new truck, a deal they struck because the family wanted him suitably registered among the faithful. I could have cried.

But this is Crystal's story, all of it—more than the council heard the night she visited to profess her faith. Some may fault me for not telling the council everything, but even the men in the room would say that there's no good reason to say some things in public if everybody can pretty much guess the whole truth anyway. Besides, the real story that night was Crystal te Lindert's joy. For too long, the people at Barneveld Calvary had seen nothing but disdain in her face—that is, if they saw her in church at all.

Because she was quite royally pregnant, her appearance was no mystery. Admission to the sacraments at Calvary Church includes, of course, the opportunity to baptize a newborn, and Crystal wasn't the first pregnant woman to enter the council room that year; surprise pregnancies often prompt righteousness. So once they saw her, the old men of the Calvary council knew her motivations—or thought they did. How many times haven't I thanked God that his Holy Spirit is a whole lot more wily than the best and brightest of our minds—Barneveld or Athens?

Crystal's eyes are pale blue, the color of the sky at the break of morning; that night they seemed guileless. Her hair is the memorable auburn shade of red that seems aflame. If twenty young women had walked in with her, Crystal's hair would have distinguished her immediately. That night it was more untended, less purposefully arranged than it had been, and the men liked that more untended look—less style, more grace.

She sat at the head of the table with me, and she answered my opening round of questions in a softer voice than any of them would have guessed, but not with her face down, as if she were afraid. She addressed each of the men with her eyes, straight on, as if to assure them each that the story she was telling was the God-sent truth.

"I have come to believe," she told them, "that who I am and what I am is something, in a way, already determined. And I don't mean to sound as if there's nothing I can do about it either—or should have done." She squinted and smiled, as if what she was explaining was a truth with the sweetness of a riddle. "I'm not proud of who I was or where I've gone wrong— not at all," she said, the only motion a slight toss of her head that one might have translated as arrogance had her words not argued otherwise. "But while I'm sorry for what I've been, sorry for my sins, I'm not sorry, in a way, for the experience, because what I've come to believe is that I wouldn't be here if I hadn't been what I was." Her eyes skipped around the table. "Does that make sense?" And then she let out a laugh, a giggle the men recognized as heavenly comic relief. "I'm ready," she said. "He's really come into my life, and now it's time for me to be something I've never been." She patted her belly. "I mean that in more ways than one." And then they chuckled.

To me, those words were a plainer form of God-reliance than had been heard in that church since the Depression, probably. Then she told them her story—most of it.

11

It begins twenty-four years ago, long before I was at Barneveld Calvary, with Crystal's birth, the daughter of Marty and Else Kamphoff. Marty Kamphoff's roots are poor, the son of a tenant farmer who spent his life leaning more heavily on the promises of God than using his arms to fork out hog pens. His folks were quiet people, devout, less concerned with the things of this world than maybe any child's parents should be, loved for their piety as much as they were pitied for their lack of business sense. When Marty had an auction sale of his folks' earthly treasures years ago, he stuck three times as much money in his pocket than his father had paid for the old Ford when he bought it, used, in 1947. They were wonderful people, rich in the Lord, sorely lacking in mammon.

Marty Kamphoff grew up poor and made himself rich in the finest tradition of the American dream. He made his fortune when he caught wind of a product that was scoring well in California: "Victor Cleaners—For a Better World." He gambled what he and his wife had, and today, a couple decades later, he sits comfortably at the peak of one grand sales pyramid. He is one of the wealthiest men in Barneveld, and all he does is send off boxed cartons of environmentally sound cleaning agents to teams of slavish sales reps poised to peddle those squeaky clean products to zealots who believe the CEO of Procter and Gamble is really Satan the tempter. Just enough religion to make him rich.

Barneveld people don't mistrust Marty simply because he has money, although they're capable of that kind of jealousy. They'd say you can dry it, stick it in pellets, freeze it, or turn it into bean soup, by golly, but when you get it up to your nose it's still manure—that's what they'd say about Marty Kamphoff.

All of this, we didn't talk about at all the night Crystal made her profession. All of this, of course, most everyone knows. But all of it, really, is part of Crystal's profession.

If you'd grown up here, you'd likely say that's the whole story. But there's more.

On a windy night a dozen or so years ago at Watertower Park, a special baseball game was played before a huge crowd. Crystal te Lindert, then thirteen and going on twenty-one, as people said, kept the scorebook for her father. Marty Kamphoff was coaching the Morey Bees, a bunch of African-American kids from Mississippi. Among them was Cedrick Myles, a tall and gangly eleven-year-old with a cannon for an arm.

The year the Morey Bees were up, Marty Kamphoff was into mopeds. When they weren't playing ball, those kids from Mississippi were buzzing all over town, advertising Kamphoff's newest gimmick. The cops let them be—they were visitors, after all.

Everybody remembers how hard the wind blew the night they played an all-star lineup of Barneveld Little Leaguers, how the wind raised dust all over the infield and blew grit into everyone's eyes. People remember Cedrick, the biggest kid, looking over at the dugout from first base and yelling, "Coach, let me pitch." And they remember Marty Kamphoff, not regarding him, trying to keep his cap on his head while pointing down at the scorebook his red-haired daughter held tightly in her hands. "Just throw strikes, Tad! Just throw strikes!" Kamphoff yelled, as if death by home runs was preferable to white kids trotting home from third base on a succession of walks.

What some even remember is the way the kid named Tad chucked the ball into his glove, then stepped to the rubber before delivering another dead-bird pitch. He was starting to aim the ball, and every pitch came more and more from the side—a sure sign his arm was shot. Between pitches he didn't even move his shoulder.

Now Barneveld people may not understand the poetry of T. S. Eliot, but they know how to read a kid with a sore arm; and what Cedrick likely never understood was that the crowd knew, just like he did, that his buddy shouldn't be on the mound.

What's worse, the crowd knew far too much about Marty Kamphoff's motivations. Marty had brought up all these kids from the Mississippi Delta, set up a series of ball games in the area, and asked for donations for a medical clinic. It was noble work. But doing good, after all, is a lot like pitching—it's all in the spin, and Marty's been mixing up spitters with his other pitches since he was old enough to stand up and be seen on Main Street. What he was doing that night was letting the white kids win a game they probably wouldn't have unless he threw it. Credit him with this: He wanted to make big money for his special project, and he figured he'd do better if the fans were happy that their kids—the white kids—could beat out any team of black scrubs. In Watertower Park that night, nobody was a bigger racist than Marty Kamphoff, the man who'd brought all these black kids up north.

The problem with people like Marty—big money, little brains—is that they really believe the rest of the world is as dumb as they can be. He threw the game, and we all knew it— so did Cedrick Myles, who likely understood the deception in a whole different way. All he knew right then was that his buddy's arm was gone and his team was in danger of losing to a bunch of kids who shouldn't have won. So right then, he did something nobody forgot because it was, to the entire crowd, a brash act of public and not-so-civil disobedience. The kid knew Tad shouldn't be pitching.

"Let me pitch," Cedrick said when he walked over to the mound.

Tad slapped the ball into his glove a couple times. "I can hardly lift my arm."

Cedrick Myles looked over at the dugout, then swiped the ball out of his buddy's glove and slapped Tad on the butt with his trapper, sending him to first. The whole crowd went into a hush as the big kid delivered the ball to the plate with the kind of speed only a machine could measure.

The first three times Kamphoff yelled, Cedrick pretended to be deaf and kept delivering warm-up pitches. Then he twisted his wrist to signal the big curve and bent one halfway around the county in that stiff Iowa wind.

"Myles, get back to first!" Kamphoff screamed and came after him. Now Marty doesn't know much about baseball, but he long ago understood how to act in public. All that mattered to him was politics and power, and he knew that Cedrick's disobedience was his own public humiliation. Pride pushed him, and racism.

"Give me the ball," he growled when he got to the mound.

Cedrick wouldn't look at him. He kept right on throwing. "Tad ain't got a thing left in his arm," he said.

"I make the rules," Kamphoff told him. "You aren't going to tell me what to do."

Cedrick swallowed the ball in his trapper. He didn't spit or rant or rave, but neither did he give up quickly.

"Give me the ball," Marty said again. "I don't want to take you down right here in front of all these people."

The whole crowd heard those words. Marty said them almost proudly, in fact. Cedrick Myles, already as tall as Marty, turned all the way around on the mound, put his back to Marty Kamphoff, and stared out at center field, the ball behind him in one cocked fist. Then in one swift motion, he spiked that ball into the dirt behind the mound and marched back to first base.

While few remember the score or the fact that Barneveld won, everyone remembers the game. But my guess is that Cedrick Myles may well be the only one there who certifiably *can't* forget.

Perhaps it is a mark of my lack of faith that I find it difficult to say what I must at this point, because to my mind, what happened next is a special kind of providence. Cedrick Myles, the big kid from the Mississippi Delta, came back to play a role in Crystal's pilgrimage, and, unless one figures in the mysterious will of God, that would seem most unlikely. But it happened.

Today, Cedrick Myles stands six feet, six inches tall. He lives in Cedar Rapids, where just last season he led the Hoover University basketball team to a second-place finish in the Valley Conference and a bid in the NCAA. He's a star, and in Barneveld, everybody knows his name. They've watched his box scores for four years.

Several months ago, after Hoover lost in the play-offs, Cedrick Myles got a call from a man who introduced himself as Marty Kamphoff. I never heard the conversation, but others did—Marty set it up in a public way, as he so often did. Would Cedrick and a couple of his Hawk buddies like to come up to Barneveld for a benefit basketball game? Kamphoff was sure people would come out because they all remembered the summer when those kids from Mississippi took over Barneveld streets. "Remember how you guys flew around on my mopeds?" he asked. "Everybody's been watching you for all these years at Hoover. I thought maybe we could arrange a little homecoming."

Cedrick didn't say much at first.

"C of C's putting up a flower garden next door to the city offices—right downtown," Kamphoff told him. "It's for next year's centennial. Proceeds go to that."

"I'll have to check with the guys," Cedrick said. "It's a long way across the state."

"People here got big hearts—you know that," Kamphoff said. "By the way, no Sundays, right? You remember that?"

"That's right," Cedrick said. "You people are all Christians."

"Tradition up here," Kamphoff said, chuckling away the silliness.

The only people surprised by the size of the crowd that night were the Hoover visitors. The place was jammed. Kids sat on the stage and pulled their feet up beneath them. At the baseline on the south side, a line of single guys stood the whole night long, one foot up behind them against the mats on the walls. The stands were packed. From behind the scorekeeper's table, Marty Kamphoff stood several times at the start, microphone in hand, trying to urge the crowd to shove together and make more room for the people still coming in from the parking lot.

"Welcome back, Cedrick," said a big sign someone had hung from the gallery of state championship banners along the ceiling rafters.

Little Barneveld's huge gym holds fifteen hundred people. The school itself is quite new, but teachers often criticize the planning committee for lack of foresight—no central library, for instance, and no large group facility other than the gym. But the gym is a palace. The retractable bleachers on the balconies on both sides allow three high school teams to practice at once. A four-sided scoreboard hangs from the ceiling—just like the one at Madison Square Garden.

That night Cedrick Myles took bloody revenge on the place where his Little League team got beat. He scored forty points, dished out ten assists, pulled down more than a dozen boards, but most importantly, brought the house down a half-dozen times with a series of acrobatic dunks, including a dazzling behind-the-head stunner off an alley-oop on a fast break. The game was not exactly a rout, although people knew it could have been. The Hawks turned the contest into an exhibition about eight minutes or so into the second half.

But the game was not itself as significant to Crystal's story as what happened afterward.

Cedrick Myles was the last to get to the shower that night because everyone who is anyone in Barneveld muscled his way over to talk to the big star after the game. The mayor himself pumped Cedrick's arm as if it were a slot machine, and Marty, not to be outdone, gave him a bear hug, despite the fact that Cedrick still glistened with sweat.

Crystal hugged Cedrick too, even though he had to be reminded that she was Marty's daughter—the redhead who had kept the book in the dugout during that Little League tour long ago. With her arms around Cedrick, she told him that he and his friends were invited to a little party on an acreage four miles west of the baseball field. "We'll leave the lights on," she told him, dipping her eyebrows. "Besides, you won't be able to miss it for all the cars." She squeezed him. "You're coming then?" she encouraged.

"It's going to take a while," he told her, nodding at the lineup still facing him.

"We'll party long," she said warmly. "Come anytime."

One of the Hoover guys is married and didn't go. Sam Whitley, the point guard, smelled a rat and stayed behind; his teammates used to kid him a lot about being stuck with his father's Pentecostal Christianity. Jerome Jefferson drove home to Omaha as soon as he had showered. So only four Hoover stars went—Cedrick Myles; Marshall Montrose, a power forward; Jeff Briscoe, a linebacker from the Hoover football team they'd brought along for a sub; and Scott Foreman, the only white guy, a native Iowan.

Crystal te Lindert and her husband, Butch, live in the house her poor Kamphoff grandparents used to own—four small rooms downstairs, three tiny bedrooms upstairs, accessible only by a narrow stairway so steep you have to be part mountain goat to get up and down. It has a modernized kitchen her father put in before the wedding and a huge sound system controlled from the living room, the only room in the house big enough to hold a dozen dancers. I'm told the kegs stand on the kitchen table during the winter; in the summer, they're outside.

I wasn't at the party—seems preachers aren't invited. Part of what I'm about to say comes from Crystal, part from her husband, part from pure conjecture. Just because I'm a preacher doesn't mean people tell me all the truth either.

I do know this: Something changes in men like Butch when superior males appear. No matter how macho they can swagger otherwise, they instantly cow. The moment the Hoover guys arrived, Butch and his friends started pitching up lobs for their special guests to rip, sweet questions meant to dramatize their worship of guys whose poster portraits kids all over Barneveld tack up in their bedrooms.

"That second half stuff—over Bleeker? That was some jam," Butch said once Cedrick was sitting. "That alley-oop, wow!"

It's a kind of flirtation really. "Whitley," Butch said, "what a magician!"

Montrose stood against the sink, and Foreman hoisted himself on the counter. Briscoe sat beside Cedrick, and they all talked basketball—the game against Ohio, double overtime, the loss to DePaul in the tournament. And according to Butch—he told me this when Crystal wasn't around—everything would have been fine if it hadn't been for the women, who slowly started wandering into the kitchen and taking places wherever they could find a corner. Crystal began doing exactly what Butch had started—tossing up sweet little comments like alley-oop passes for the stars to jam on home.

"Remember how we used to fly around town on those mopeds, Cedrick?" she said. "That was such a great time that summer—did you know I always had a crush on you?"

Cedrick looked up at her standing there, drink in hand, and winked.

The people there probably knew Butch hated the way she led Cedrick on, something she had a habit of doing once she started drinking, as they all had been that night.

19

"So, Cedrick, you going to get filthy rich in the NBA?" she asked.

According to Butch, that question ruined everything, because every male around that table knew Cedrick was not going to be drafted, and they all knew why: He couldn't hit a three-pointer. Every male around that table knew Crystal should never have put him into that embarrassing position, having to admit publicly, after the spectacular show he'd just put on, what everyone knew and nobody wanted to believe .

Something broke in the star's face, and he shrugged his shoulders. "We'll have to wait and see," he said, looking down at his beer.

"I'm so proud," Crystal said. "I used to ride on the back of his moped." She was wearing a vest, gray and silver, over a dark blue turtleneck. "When I see you on TV," she said, "I can tell my kids 'I knew him when he was a boy. He's going to be a big star, and I once had the hots for him.'" And then, "Hey," she said, "I want to dance. I want to be able to tell my kids someday that I danced with Cedrick Myles." She put her hand over his arm.

"My knees are killing me," Cedrick said.

"I'll make it slow," she told him. "We don't want these guys going back to Hoover saying Barneveld doesn't know how to party. Come on, Cedrick," she said, pulling him to his feet— typical Crystal, the old Crystal, the one we rarely saw in church.

Cedrick wasn't interested. "What's your old man going to say?" he said, as if it were a joke. What he meant, I believe, was her father, the Little League coach who'd hauled him off the mound when Cedrick could have won the game years ago. But everyone else assumed he meant Butch, who was standing right there as his often-estranged wife poured herself over the star.

"I don't care," she said, maybe the very worst words she could have said right then—not a trace of profanity or vulgarity, but something much, much worse to her husband's ears. Everybody heard it, he says. Then Crystal pulled Cedrick Myles into the tiny living room.

It would be nice to think that whatever happened that night wouldn't have happened if Cedrick had known Crystal was married to the barrel-chested mason in the cutoff Iowa State sweatshirt. But my guess is that Cedrick Myles had other reasons to come on to this woman who was coming on to him, reasons dredged up from the memory of a ball thrown angrily in the dirt at Watertower Park. He likely had his own objectives, and they probably had less to do with passion than with power.

And what about Crystal? According to her, Cedrick Myles is the only African-American at whom she'd ever taken aim, but he certainly wasn't the only male—before *or* after her marriage to Butch te Lindert.

Once it was clear that she had drawn her sights on him, Butch left the house rather than suffer more public humiliation. He says he took a bottle of vodka along to inflate his courage, and drove out on the country roads with it parked between his legs. He says he rode around and around, revving his hate.

Back at the house, a keg had been emptied. When Butch finally returned, the place was full of people—so many that no one really noticed him until he punched the power on the stereo and screamed words I'm not about to tell you here.

Even though his bloodstream was pumped with vodka, he hadn't drunk enough to make him forget the size of Cedrick Myles. Once he found the two of them in the bedroom, he took the path of least resistance and went after his wife.

I'm not about to go through the blow-by-blow because I don't believe anybody remembers exactly what happened that night, but the accounts people give are consistent on at least two points. When Cedrick intervened, he took the high moral ground, defending Crystal, who, strong as she is, is no match physically for her husband. The second point of agreement is that somewhere in the middle, it was Butch who used the "n" word. And then all was lost, although what began at that moment ended less than three minutes later.

The cops arrived, one of the women having called them in the heat of the early exchange. The cops knew the address. They'd been there often enough before.

So many years ago I can hardly remember, no seminary profs ever told me I'd find myself in the middle of a war between Butch te Lindert, who's never aspired to sainthood, and his wife Crystal, who spent the early years of her marriage waltzing along gingerly toward Vanity Fair. It seems to me now, twenty-some years of preaching later, that there's room somewhere for the whole story of Crystal's pilgrimage, her whole story. Maybe that's why I'm telling it.

What should come as no surprise to you now is something few in Barneveld know or even suspect—that in the long months Crystal was pregnant with the child she was carrying that night in the consistory room, she didn't know for sure whether she was going to deliver another Cedrick or another Butch. And it was no easy pregnancy anyway. At seven months she was having contractions, sometimes as often as four or five every half hour. In her job as a hairdresser, she stood most of the time, and Dr. Howells, noting the fact that she was prematurely dilated and effaced, ordered her to bed to fight off the effects of gravity and stress—stress he couldn't even begin to understand at that point.

Butch's story is worth noting in passing too, for he waited on his wife like a servant during those weeks—cooked and washed linens, even scrubbed the floors of the old Kamphoff house. He did everything one might expect of a hero and more—became a doting husband few would have ever believed.

Such things happen. Even though I've been through enough sessions with Butch to understand the growth of a commitment he'd never really made when he'd said his vows, I don't know to this day whether he understood his wife's anxiety during those months. I don't know that it was my place to explain it to him. I advised Crystal to do so, even told her I'd be there when she did, but I don't know if she ever acted on my advice.

Butch is a mason in town, gone all day; he also feeds hogs on a couple of acreages, so he's got chores after work. That left Crystal home alone, and even though they've got cable and a video library you wouldn't believe, she has enough of her father the hustler in her to get frustrated at the total rest Dr. Howells demanded. In the last two months she did not leave the house often—she was concerned about the baby—but she did visit every corner of that little house.

Upstairs, three bedrooms are lined up like bunks, one to the left, two to the right, each room with its own door. Perhaps because the little place has no attic, the third bedroom—the one at the front of the house—became an attic. There, among the artifacts of Kamphoff history, the clutter her father figured couldn't bring a buck at the auction sale, Crystal found a shoebox full of letters written by her grandmother to her grandfather, most of them dated 1935.

When Crystal was in high school, it never dawned on her that she was there to get an education, so she was only vaguely aware of the Depression. When she read those letters, it bothered her that she had no clue why her grandfather would be away from his family, because obviously, from what Grandma wrote, there was no war. What she heard in those lines were strange voices from people she never really knew. They were love letters, but without passion, she thought at first. There was no sense of danger in them, only a deep wish for Henry (her grandpa) to be back home with his wife and kids. He was off in Minnesota, she found out, working with Roosevelt's

23

WPA, a fact his son Marty's right-wing revisionism long ago hacked out of the family tree.

That shoebox was packed full. By mid-November not much heat reached the front bedroom, since the whole upstairs was warmed only by a grate near the steps. But for a long time Crystal simply couldn't bring that box of letters downstairs to her room, the room where she'd taken Cedrick Myles. So she read them all upstairs in the cold.

This is what she told the elders of Barneveld Calvary. She sat down in the consistory room and explained it all as if it were happening even as she spoke. And this is what we saw, all of us, in our minds, as she told us—this otherwise darlingly pampered dame, her red hair set more plain and straight than most of us had ever seen, her pregnancy obviously heavy, but her spirit as tenacious and fresh as it had ever been, sitting upstairs, absorbed by letters penned on paper so thin she had trouble deciphering the words from the loops and curls cut by the fountain pen on the opposite side of the page. She sat reading them as if they were Scripture, and in a way they *were* the words of God.

What she told me, but didn't tell the old men of the church, was that she'd been thinking often about the child being Cedrick's. That possibility was there always through those nine months, as omnipresent as the whir of the furnace fan, the only other sound in the old house. She's no more a racist than any of us, and she wasn't thinking of how hard life might be for a mixed-race child in a lily-white town. She wasn't thinking only of herself, of what a little black kid would display to the world about her sin. Crystal had never feigned much Christianity—she'd already seen enough of that in her father. What obsessed her was the thought that this movement in her, this pressing weight against her insides, had resulted from a union that, once accomplished, meant absolutely nothing to her. At some moments in the isolation of her pregnancy, what brought her almost to tears was the vision of this soon-to-be human being forever carrying the legacy of her careless seduction of Cedrick Myles.

In my estimation, she'd come in her own way to understand deeply what she'd done—its profound gravity, something that would affect later generations. And it was in that context that she read her grandma's letters.

Not once, however, did she find mention of her father. Uncle Ed was there, going fishing for the first time; Aunt Bess dressed the cats in her doll clothes; Uncle Marion was busy with a tree house; and sometimes Aunt Margaret's questions drove her mother crazy. But there was no mention of Marty.

Crystal told the church council what she had calculated quickly in her mind; her father was born in 1935 and his birthday was in December, just a week or so before Christmas. That's when she had figured out that her father wasn't around yet—that Grandma was pregnant when those letters were written. She said she flipped through the dates on the letters as if they were trading cards—many of them written when her grandma must have been just as pregnant as Crystal was herself, and just as alone—no, not as alone, not with four kids all over the house, *this* house, inside *these* walls, sitting right here somewhere.

At that moment, she said a chill ran through her as ghosts emerged from every corner, creating the sense that she wasn't alone. She wasn't afraid, however, because although the letters spoke with a voice she'd never heard before, it was the voice of her own grandmother. The letters were written weekly, on Sunday afternoons or evenings, a fact she gleaned from Grandma's recitation of what passages the preacher had used for sermons: "Dominie on 1 Peter 2:9. 'But ye are a chosen generation, a royal priesthood, an holy nation, a peculiar people; that ye should shew forth the praises of him who hath called you out of darkness into his marvelous light.'"

And then, every week, there was Grandma's little application: "How hard it is sometimes to make our lives shine for him." Just a single line of comment meant not so much to preach to her husband as to observe the truths of life she knew very well he shared.

And the afternoon service: "Dominie on the catechism. 'How great are our sins and miseries.'" And then, "Yeah, Henry, we don't have to look far either, do we?"

A week later: "Dominie on Psalm 73:1–3. 'Truly God is good to Israel, even to such as are of a clean heart. But as for me, my feet were almost gone; my steps had well nigh slipped. For I was envious at the foolish, when I saw the prosperity of the wicked.'" And then, "How blessed we are, really, with our health. Here, everything is fine this week. We have so much cause to thank the Lord. Tomatoes could use some sun. We have had too much rain. I miss you."

All Crystal remembered of her grandparents was their miserliness, her grandma's reprimand when she'd watch her grandchildren let too much water from the tap go down the drain as they waited for its temperature to cool. These people, the young married couple in the letters, were people she'd never known.

"Afternoon, Dominie on infant baptism. How our children being heirs of sin also stand in need of God's grace and thus must be baptized." And then, "Even this one, Henry—sometimes he wrestles inside like Jacob." And then the news. "Ed busy with kites all week—good, stiff winds for him too. Bess and Margaret played school sitting on bushel baskets."

For three days Crystal went into the cold upstairs and read through those letters, she said, one after another. She kept them locked upstairs, as if there were no place for them downstairs, where she lived her life. She'd wrap herself in a blanket, she told the elders, sitting up to read as if she hadn't heard the doctor's warning.

Three weeks before the baby would be born, she was lying on the couch in the living room while the house sat in silence around her—no talk shows, no local news, no soaps. She was quietly waiting for a birth she had all kinds of reasons to be anxious about. She pulled on her slippers, she said, thinking that she'd go back upstairs and read through some letters again, even though she'd been through them already, even though she'd realized how little of life her grandmother seemed to know, other than the flower bed and her children's morning play. When she thought of it—her own grandmother sitting right here in this house in a time without parties and cheating and all the horrors that had made her own life so hard to live—she wanted to read more, she said. She wanted to read them again. She thought she'd start over again—at the front of the shoebox—because the voices in the letters had become not simply the only voices in the house through the long hours she was sentenced to inactivity, but the voices that gave her hope.

So she stood up from the couch slowly, the child getting heavier and lower within her, and she told herself that this time she would take those letters downstairs instead of visiting them the way she had been doing, alone in the cold with no place to lie down. But it seemed somehow inappropriate and even wrong to have those letters on the main floor beside the huge TV and the mega-bass sound system. What Grandma wrote, she thought, should have been in a museum or a church library, a place where they could be protected from the ravages of dust and time and life itself, some sacred place where they could be reverenced.

At that moment, something fierce and unsettling rose from within her, almost as if from the child itself, something roiling like heartburn, and yet not a sickness either; something that tightened her lungs and constricted her breathing, something like an allergy that pinched every nerve in her face. She reached for the tissues and sat back down, as if whatever it was were an attack that would pass. She said she felt her skin being turned inside out, every vital organ exposed, as if an alien power suddenly had the keys to every nerve in her system.

It had to do with those letters, she said, and the fact that they were upstairs. She had this sense that she had to bring them down into her life, so she gathered her strength again, raised herself from the couch, and went to the stairs. She pressed her hand up against the wall to steady herself, then took hold of the rail on the left side, put her right hand up against the wall, and started slowly climbing.

Once upstairs, she opened the door of the attic bedroom, kept herself straight with one hand on the wall, and picked up the box. She put it beneath her arm—almost like a football, she told the old men, smiling at the joke—and then turned and left, swinging the door closed and locked behind her.

The stairs in that old house are vicious, so steep there's little to distinguish them from a ladder. At the bottom is a sharp twist so jagged the individual steps narrow to no more than a few inches as they sweep the corner. No one would build a house like that today. And Crystal was weak, the doctor's own warning in her ears, telling her to stay down. She descended the stairs, the shoebox full of her grandmother's letters between her arm and her side, her knees limp as if she'd continuously caught her weight from a walk down a long, steep hill. At the turn at the bottom, she steadied herself with a hand up on the ceiling, put her shoulder against the wall, and came off the final steps, her right foot reaching for stability, her left following in the unmistakable pattern of an old woman.

When she stood at the foot of the stairs, she breathed deeply and shut the door behind her. It wasn't so much of a rescue, she said, as another kind of birth, this taking the letters into her home, into the scene of so much she'd come to regret. She said that God had brought something into her life from an attic bedroom, something she was simply going to have to make room for.

She sat on the couch and rested her elbow on the armrest, then laid down her head, the box there under her arm. She couldn't say exactly what was happening in her, why her strength seemed gone. If it was the beginning of labor, she felt that there was no way she had the power to carry it through. If the baby were to come now, she thought, the whole business would have to be accomplished without her.

Tears came—even in the recitation there before the elders. She said she wanted Butch but knew he was at work. Besides, how would she explain? She prayed for the first time since she'd been pregnant, for the first time in many years, she said. She lay on that couch where she'd spent so much time, and she prayed in groans and sadness, her head down on her arm, as if there were no way of explaining anything to God but with the sound of her sadness.

She felt her heart race, but there was no movement inside her, no sense of a birth beginning. Deliberately, she pulled herself upright on the couch and told herself that it wasn't the child striking terror, for it was something like terror she felt, some deep fear.

With both hands, she grabbed the shoebox and lowered it into her lap. Then she felt something quell in her, the sharp points of her shoulder blades receding into the sheath of her back. Her breath steadied, her shoulders lowered, her arms fell, and the box on her lap seemed almost like an anvil, something that wouldn't shake. What she'd taken from the attic, something she didn't know how to name, was something that brought her peace.

That was the story she told the elders in the church the night she came to profess her faith.

There are old men in Barneveld Calvary, old men with years and years of life experience on this broad patch of Iowa farmland. But none of them had ever heard a story quite like Crystal's.

When the baby came, Sarah Ann, she was Butch's daughter—pale blue eyes, hairless, the same button nose. Butch has been beaming ever since.

For Crystal not to have felt some relief would be to make her the kind of saint no one is; but she was sure, the moment she went into labor, that she would have loved that child no matter what its pigmentation.

You may not believe her story. You may think Crystal te Lindert's religious experience was simply a physical manifestation of the suppression of her worst fears, her latent racism, and her guilt over what she'd done with Cedrick Myles. But the elders bought the whole story—every bit of it—even though they didn't know the Cedrick Myles connection. They said, as did many, that the phenomenon Crystal came to label as her conversion was exactly what she claims it to be. "Praise God!" they said, and then they prayed.

You may choose what you think, but I know what I believe.

Duane Foxhoven's Trees for Tomorrow

What happened decades ago between Barneveld's most famous pastor, the Reverend Cecil Meekhof, and Duane Foxhoven's father created a bruise on Duane's soul that only deepened as, one by one, those few who knew the old story died and left him alone with the memory. For close to forty years, according to his wife, every time he saw the Reverend Meekhof, a jolt of something not unlike electric current coursed through his body so violently that it became difficult for him to hold the cigarette he was rarely without.

That's why Duane was shocked when the good Reverend Meekhof called to ask him to landscape the new home he and his wife had built at the eastern edge of Barneveld. Even though Duane felt that Reverend Meekhof had changed the course of his father's life—and his own—the two men hadn't spoken once during the years they'd lived side by side.

Foxhoven himself would likely never speak to me, but then he speaks very little, not even to his wife, she says. I don't think I'm wrong when I say that no one really knows Duane Foxhoven's mind. What we know is at least something of his acts, and although I may be altering the Gospel text by using it in this way, I'm assuming that when Christ said that by their fruits you shall know them, he gave me some license to tell this story.

Foxhoven shouldn't have been surprised at Meekhof's request to do his landscaping. He had built a good business—twelve full-time, seasonal employees putting in ornamental bushes and shrubs, laying sod, digging up old yards to put in sprinkling systems—basic residential landscaping. The old retired preacher called because the business was good, reputable.

They talked no longer than two minutes. The Reverend's back wasn't what it was, he said, chuckling, but he'd like to get something in the ground yet, before the heat of summer—could he count on it, even though he should have called mid-winter, when the new house was going up? The old man never said a word about anything other than shrubbery, and my guess is that Foxhoven assumed the old preacher was afraid to talk about what had happened years ago, even humiliated. He likely appreciated what he thought of as the old man's suffering.

"I'll be there yet this afternoon," he told the preacher. "I'll come myself. You'll be there?"

"I've got golf at three," Meekhof said. "What else has a retired minister got to do? We're the only house out here—there aren't any neighbors to preach to yet." The old man was trying to humor him.

"I can get there before that," Duane told him.

An hour later Duane parked the truck on the street out front of Meekhof's, then glanced at the new castle, his heart drumming as he mashed the cigarette butt in the scattered remains of a hundred others in the tray. He took his cap off the seat beside him, snugged it over his head, and grabbed the clipboard from the hook on the dash. The only words in his mind were a litany of obscenities he repeated like a mantra lest he forget what he thought of the sweet old liver-spotted preacher everyone loved.

He stepped from the truck and assessed the yard. That spring, rain was in short supply, and the broken ground around the new house lay in thick chunks of hard clay. He made a mental note of how much black dirt they'd have to truck in while Meekhof—dressed in green walking shorts, a short-sleeved shirt, and crew socks beneath his sandals—moved slowly down the new spotless driveway.

"Reverend," Duane said, eyes on the clipboard.

"Everybody says you do good work," the preacher commented.

"I'm not about to argue," he said, sketching in circles and lines.

Meekhof crossed his arms over his chest. "I'd love to do this work myself," he said. "Time was, I *would* have too, but back then I was too busy with the church." He pointed toward the house. "What we're looking at is something nice in there. The wife wants flowers, but I told her they were going to be *her* burden—even though Scripture says that ever since the fall, tending the garden belongs to men."

That's the kind of line the old man is famous for, but he told me that not once in that few minutes of assessment did Duane Foxhoven even crack a smile. A preacher learns to read an audience, and what he saw in Duane's face at first looked like pure boredom, but later drew up closer to hate.

"We're not paupers either," Meekhof told him, "but I'm not going to invest a fortune into this. I got ten years, at best—Bible says fourscore and ten—or was it Lincoln said that?" He looked around. "I suppose it's a good thing though, isn't it?"

"What's that?" Foxhoven said absently.

"Putting your money in trees and shrubs. There's something selfless about it, don't you think? Putting in growing things when you're my age—planting trees whose shade I'll never sit in."

Foxhoven jotted down some notes.

"Course there is—and you ought to say it too," Meekhof told him. "It's a good line. You can use it for your business. Marketing—that's the name of the game today, isn't it?" He put a hand on the truck window. "You ought to sell your business that way," he said. "'Trees for Tomorrow'—call it something catchy like that."

"That's clever," Foxhoven said, surveying the front of the house.

"Go ahead and use it if you want," the preacher told him. "Your name is Foxhoven, isn't it?"

"Duane Foxhoven."

"You ought to pitch the whole business that way, Foxhoven. There's something wonderful about planting trees, especially out here in Iowa." He waved at the monstrous sky. "Make it your logo or something—'Trees for Tomorrow'—something like that. A man can make money on faith out here among all these Christian people." He waved his finger. "Not that I ever did." He reached over his shoulder to scratch his back. "What I learned in this town," he said, "it's amazing. I came here from New Jersey. Never been out to the Plains before, but I said to the wife that this town looked like the kind of place with promise. Good people, just needed some direction."

Duane sketched in a few circles up around the base of the house.

"You know, people will do the right thing if you just give them the right context." He pointed, as if there were some imaginary audience. "I grew up a preacher's kid. I had two uncles who were preachers, and half the time when I was a kid we had preachers over for dinner. I always told myself when I got old I was going to learn to keep my trap shut so I didn't turn into one of those old motor mouths, and now look at me go on and on."

Duane shrugged his shoulders.

"I should have been a landscaper," Meekhof said, "putting in 'Trees for Tomorrow.' Of course, lots of people would have rather had me planting trees too," he said, jokingly. "Where is it you go to church, Foxhoven?"

"Don't go much," Duane said, twisting his neck slightly as if it were sore. "Wife does. Calvary."

"Wonderful people there," the preacher said. "Years ago, I couldn't have set foot in that church. Today they call me two, three times a year to fill the pulpit." He turned slightly, as if he could see the steeple of Calvary Church behind him. "Things change," he said, "thank the Lord."

Duane drew in an oblong flower bed beside the driveway.

"My word, here I am using up all of your precious time. You didn't come to hear a sermon either, did you?"

"Better me than my men," Foxhoven said.

"Well, what we're thinking is, this piece in here could be fully landscaped," he said, pointing at the island of broken soil between the driveway and the walk up to the front door. "What *we're* thinking—listen to me—*we!* What *my wife* is thinking is what I should say."

"A perennial garden here?" Foxhoven asked.

"She's got this thing about a wagon wheel, even though she was born no more than an hour by train from Manhattan. She thinks she's a farm girl since we've been here in Iowa so many years."

"Shrubbery around it?"

"Sure, some shrubbery. I told her I was too old to be fighting the curse of sin myself—but I told you that, didn't I? Get to be my age and you lose track of what you said ten minutes before."

Duane looked up at him. "Not that way with the old days though," he said.

"What's that?" Meekhof said.

"—with the old days." He looked up at the preacher. "You always hear that when people get old they can't remember what happened yesterday," Duane told him, "but they can't forget what happened years ago." He made a couple more squiggles on the pad. "Is that true?"

Meekhof said that for a moment he felt fear run through his nerves at the look in the man's eyes, but he didn't know why that look was there because what Duane had nudged into the conversation didn't hit home. He said he didn't remember what he should have about Duane Foxhoven and his father. All he knew was that this man was carrying something huge. He could read it in the darkness of his eyes. And then something clicked. "What'd you say your name was again?" the preacher said.

"Foxhoven."

"I know that—"

"Duane."

"Who's your father?"

"Albert," he said, "but he never went by Albert. He was a man everybody called Brush."

"Albert?" the preacher said, digesting.

"Called him 'Brush' because once upon a time he used to cut hair—but that was long before my time. Never knew him as a barber at all, just my old man. Ornery too."

"The name rings a bell—Albert," Meekhof said.

And then, "It ought to," Duane told him. "*You* baptized me."

Meekhof almost froze. "I did? You sure?" He looked for something in Duane's face that might key a memory. "Albert?" he repeated.

"If you knew him by that name, you didn't know my old man," Duane said.

"Used to be in my church?"

"Used to be—long ago."

And that was it. That was enough. They'd come close enough. Foxhoven changed the course of the conversation. "Listen," he said, "what I'll do is draw up a plan and give you an estimate over the phone. You can scratch off what you like or come up with something else, but it'll be a place to start."

He ripped the sheet off the pad and pointed up at the chunks of clay at the base of the new house. "That's all though? Just this spot here? Or do you want me to figure in some things all the way around the place?"

"Your father left my church?" Meekhof asked.

The memory of that night was so deep into Duane Foxhoven's soul that he didn't find it hard to offer the preacher something of a half-truth. "My mother hauled me to the Methodist church," he said. "But my old man always said you baptized me."

"You sure?" Meekhof said.

"I don't remember it," Duane said, and right then he smiled for the first time—if you could call it a smile.

Those few minutes out on the unfinished front yard pushed the old preacher's mind back fifty years to an event he'd nearly forgotten after all the successes of his long career in Barneveld's First Reformed Church.

By 1945, Brush Foxhoven's house, one of Barneveld's finest turn-of-the-century houses, reeked with the acrid smell of rubber. Duane's old man had stockpiled tires the day he'd gotten wind of the possibility of war rationing, filled his basement with them, in fact, and then, through the war years, sold them to people who needed them—as well as a few who didn't—for prices that inflated as steadily as everyone's wages. Brush was Barneveld's ace black marketeer.

Not until he was in his late twenties did Duane ever nail down the odd sensation he felt in Daryl Blekking's Central Tire, but one day a switch turned on his memory, and right there in the shop he recognized the discomfiting smell of his childhood. "All of a sudden," he told Daryl, "the smell in here reminds me of the war, of the place I grew up in. Odd, isn't it?"

Blekking wasn't quite sure what to say.

Duane had grown up so accustomed to that sharp odor of rubber that he became oblivious to it in his father's house. But what he never forgot was the night Reverend Meekhof came to their house with two other men. He didn't hear the conversation—at least not word for word. All he caught was the shouting, and that's what stayed in him, growing in volume year after year. This is how it went, or something like it.

"May we come in?" Meekhof said at Foxhoven's front door. He was with an elder—official business. It was December 1944.

"What do you want?" Brush asked, not without some acrimony.

"We're here from the church," the young preacher said, half turning to acknowledge the men behind him. The preacher's face was much less reddened, less blotchy than it is today, and he was thin and wiry, a formidable opponent. "We want to have a few words with you," he told Duane's father, who was no slouch.

"Ain't I gave enough?" Brush asked him.

"We'd like to discuss a matter between you and Hardwick here." He pointed behind him to Hardwick Kooiker.

"What's he done—went and told his mama?"

The young Reverend Meekhof, lately arrived in town with a sense of calling that was crystal clear, had taken upon himself the office of God's own voice in this flat and open land, and he was much more interested in overturning the tables of the money changers in this little Jerusalem than he was in turning the other cheek. He told me that back then he often saw himself cloaked in righteousness—the keeper of the keys of the kingdom.

"The man has a grievance," Meekhof told him, "and we're here following the lessons of Scripture in Matthew 18."

"You ask him if he got his crop out," Foxhoven said.

"That's not the issue—"

"The heck it ain't," Brush said, the open door in his hand.

"May we come in?" Meekhof asked again. Brush Foxhoven seemed little more than a two-bit corn-fed hood to Cecil Meekhof, who'd grown up in New Jersey, just down the block from the Mafia.

"You want to talk business, Reverend," Brush said, "you come downtown to the shop. I'll show you the receipt. I had to smuggle that stinking combine out of Canada for him, and if he thinks he got took with what I asked for it," he pointed into the silent Kooiker's face, "you tell him I'll take it back. There's a whole list of other farmers—"

"That's not the issue," the Reverend said again.

"Then what is?"

"A matter of the heart," Meekhof said. "There's some deception here—some cheating."

Brush Foxhoven spit back. "If he thinks I cheated him, tell him to go find his own combine! Tell him to go cry to the ration board when he can't get his crop out. Tell him there's a war on. Get that into his thick head."

"It's a matter of justice," the preacher said.

"Justice—"

"He says that thing broke down a dozen times—"

"I don't make 'em," Brush said. "I just find 'em for people. We all got our work, Reverend, and there ain't nothing about war time that's pretty—either over there or at home."

Meekhof said the more Brush talked, the more he seemed as full of sin as anyone he'd ever seen.

"All of a sudden I'm evil?" Brush demanded. "People you consider saints in this town are trying to get an extra book of stamps for gas from me so they can ride around on Sundays. I got people willing to trade most anything for white sugar, and you tell me *I'm* a sinner? I know women who'd pay me almost anything for a pair of nylons."

Meekhof turned to Kooiker. "You wait outside," he told him. "We'll talk to him."

All this happened not that long before Christmas—that's what Duane remembers of that night. Once, at the very beginning of their marriage, his wife says, he told her the story himself. He'd been sitting in his room, the first one on the left upstairs, up the open staircase, trying to wrap a present in newspaper. He told her how he'd heard the tough conversation downstairs, his father's snarling, and he went to the top of the stairs. He was a kid—six or seven years old—and he heard all of that biting talk.

Once the door slammed shut behind Kooiker, Meekhof moved a little closer. "People in this town say all kinds of bad things about you, and it isn't because you don't get them what they have to have. It's because you gouge people, Foxhoven."

"My business ain't your concern," Brush told him. "I'd consider it prudent of you to remember I give money to that church. And besides, there's a war on—in case you haven't heard."

"That's the point," Meekhof said.

The two of them faced off like bullies, a peach-faced preacher, full of righteousness, and Barneveld's own black market king.

"God's church has no room for thieves," Meekhof said.

"Who's writing the rules—you or the Lord?" Brush said.

"'Thou shalt not steal' are no words I ever wrote," the preacher replied.

"Get out!" Brush shouted. "You think you can keep the flock pure if I'm gone? Well, let me tell you something—you got farmers peddling meat they butcher on the sly, you know that? I got school board members who'll pay almost anything for a refrigerator—"

"The church has the responsibility—"

"Get out!" Foxhoven said again.

What Duane never forgot was the anger he heard at the bottom of the steps. He was a child, and what registered in his soul were those cutting tones.

Old Reverend Meekhof told me he had stood there facing Duane's father, begging a fight. "In our church," Meekhof told him, "you're not welcome at the Lord's Table. You hear me? Not until you learn humility in the face of authority."

That's what he told Duane's father close to half a century ago.

Once Duane heard his father's footsteps pound back through the dining room and kitchen and descend into the basement, he picked up the Christmas present he was wrapping and made his way downstairs, his still-too-big slippers flapping over his toes. He went to the living room and laid the present beneath the tree, then sat and stared at the lights, his eyes loosely focused so the whole thing seemed a wonderful blurry vision of holiday colors.

Then his mother came home, removed her coat, and hung it in the closet of the downstairs bedroom. Duane quietly walked into the dining room and lifted the glass ball ornament from the buffet, turning it upside down so the snowfall swirled over the manger scene. When his father came up from the cellar, Duane was standing just outside the kitchen, close enough to hear him say the only words his angry father ever uttered about what had just happened at the door of his house.

"We're never going back to that church," he told his wife. That was the gist of it, although there was more.

"Why?" his mother said.

"I don't want to talk about *why*. You hear me, Gladys?" he said. "We're gone."

And that's why Duane Foxhoven, who was baptized in the big church in Barneveld, grew up in Calvary, even though his family had been part of the other church for generations. They left the big church and came to Calvary, though Brush never attended with any regularity. Gladys did, setting the pattern, I suppose, for Duane's entire life, because even today while his wife, Laurie, attends with their children, I saw him only once or twice in the church I served for many years. When I asked

Laurie about him once early in my stay at that church, she simply shook her head, a warning. But a few weeks later, almost out of nowhere, she stopped in to tell me the story her husband had told her long ago—told her only once, she said, as if to say, "for all time."

Once the war ended, Brush was never happy. He'd made his bucks, and nobody in town forgot exactly how he'd done it. After ten years, his business languished, even though he'd built up a considerable fortune. But the reason for his failure was clear—he'd lost his reputation in a town where, sadly enough, reputation is synonymous with salvation.

From Christmas 1944, until the day Duane Foxhoven left his parental home, all he'd ever heard from his father—his eventually bankrupt father—was a thousand curses at the Reverend Cecil Meekhof and anybody else connected to the church. Most of that railing was said in a whine it took Duane thirty years to understand to be the result of one night of harsh words in 1944.

When Brush died one morning in January, right there in the implement dealership he'd run so successfully through the war—and so unsuccessfully afterward—everyone knew he went to the grave a bitter man, who never said a good thing to anyone, even his family, and especially his son.

Not all of the story is ancient history. In a town as small as Barneveld, people can run away from each other, but never much farther than a backyard.

The police brought Duane's oldest son home early one morning a week after he'd drawn up the preacher's estimates. They brought Scott in, drunk, having found him in a car he'd been driving without a license. The kid hadn't had a license for more than a year, not since the second time he'd been caught drunk and driving illegally. This was the third time. He was only nineteen.

Scott's situation was so hopeless that he did the most opportune thing and threw himself on the mercy of the law. To show his brokenness, he asked to be admitted—that morning yet—even before his court appearance, to a detox center. "I'd rather sit there than somewhere else," he told his parents and the cops who stood there beside him with their caps under their arms. "I'm going nowhere anyway," he said. So Duane and Laurie Foxhoven drove their oldest son to the hospital.

There must be a special place in heaven for spouses like Laurie Foxhoven, who learn early on in a marriage that their place has very definite lines. She says she knew she couldn't say much with her husband there, knew by experience. But Duane Foxhoven never learned a thing about being a father. With just the three of them, and Laurie not about to open up, father and son talked, maybe for the first time in three years. Scott had been hip-deep in trouble by the time he was fourteen.

The road to the city is double laned, so you can put the car on cruise and do little more than steer. But the Foxhovens had been out of town for a long time before anything meaningful came up.

"You really *have* to drink?" Duane asked his son. "Is it that kind of thing with you? You can't live without booze?"

"I got to do something," Scott told him, a sweatshirt tied around his shoulders. He coughed hard, several times, even as he smoked. "It's going to be twenty years before I can drive."

"Should have thought of that last night," Duane said.

There's always a cop in the Coop gas station in both of the small towns on the way to the city, so Duane slowed the car, almost by instinct. "What I can't understand is how you get the beer all the time. People are supposed to be cracking down."

"It's no sweat," he said.

"Somebody get it for you, or what?"

"I can't buy. Shoot, everybody knows me."

"You hire somebody?"

Then Scott spit out a name that made Laurie cringe. "Andy Meekhof bought it," he said, bringing his arm up to rub beneath his nose.

Andy Meekhof, as you've probably guessed, is the good Reverend's grandson.

The hospital was a miserable place, tile floors smashed with cigarette butts, unshaved patients in baggy robes, fat women sitting with hunched shoulders, their thick legs flattened beneath them on old church benches. The man in charge had received a note from the police telling them a kid was coming from Barneveld, so the Foxhovens were expected.

Once Scott was checked in and it was time for Duane and Laurie to leave, there was no great show of emotion between father and son. Laurie tried to hug her boy, but he was cold as steel.

The man in charge said they'd call if Scott needed something but that they shouldn't figure on talking again for at least a week—no calls, no visits. That was part of the therapy. They'd call when his parents could visit, the man said. Laurie said she waited until she was at home to cry.

Meanwhile, what glowed in Duane's soul like nuclear waste was the name his son had spit out, the buyer of the booze that got his son drunk and once more in court—and that buyer's name was Andy Meekhof.

Now the fact that Andy Meekhof was buying beer for Scott Foxhoven would not lay a hush over morning coffee in the bowling alley downtown, because everybody knew Andy was no cherub. Some of the guys would shake their heads, maybe pitying Andy's esteemed grandpa for yet another sting on the family reputation. But who knows if the charge was true? Scott Foxhoven was, after all, hardly a reliable witness.

Nevertheless, Duane's mind was already busy with what had climbed to the top of his work schedule—the job at the old preacher's new house. So he went to the job site that day, carrying a prophetic urge rivaling anything Jeremiah ever lugged through old Israel. He went there prepared to assault the good Reverend with the tarnished truth of his grandson's life. His plans for the conversation were as thoughtfully designed as the blueprint he'd drawn up for landscaping the triangle between the driveway and the front walk. All he needed was an opening.

He'd had one of his guys come by earlier in the week with the skid loader to grade out the area, then put some black dirt down for a base. Finishing the whole thing wasn't really that big of a job, certainly nothing he couldn't handle. But the guys at the shop must have been surprised when he announced that morning he was doing it alone. In late May, even before school gets out, there is so much work around the shop—customers and landscaping plans—that Duane rarely gets his hands dirty. But this one, he claimed, was his.

He loaded all the stuff on his own pickup—bushes, shrubs, flowers, and the umbrella-like pagoda dogwood he'd planned as the centerpiece. What he'd designed for the Reverend and his wife was very nice and not inexpensive. Somehow, I think he actually might have enjoyed drawing the plans up, might have even considered sabotaging the whole place by designing something really ugly to emerge after a year or two. But he put such childishness behind him and began plotting out a way to bring some beauty to Meekhof's new front yard—to do the right thing, you might say, in a kind of righteous spite, taking the moral high ground on the esteemed old preacher. In his mind, however, he was ready to pay back the old man.

He parked the truck out front, unloaded the rolls of plastic first, then the bundles—three crimson pygmy barberries for a line up close to the foundation; five goldflame spirea for a bed beside the driveway; two miniature arcade junipers to punctuate the arcadias he'd lay in a long swoop up from the sidewalk; enough tulips and geraniums for two flower rings; and of course, the pagoda dogwood.

The dirt was soft and fine, so he followed his own footprints back out toward the truck to pick up the spade, then stopped at the street to check the whole triangle for balance of depth and color.

Even planting shrubbery demands an eye for the future. You really can't assess the whole place by the pots standing on the bare ground; you have to envision what the setting is going to be once the dogwood gets up ten or twelve feet, once the junipers creep out over the stone bark and cover what space they eventually would—once the Reverend was parked finally in the cemetery. I know. Duane did our lawn not long ago. I watched him work. Everything was methodical and exact.

The first time he was at the Meekhofs', he'd asked the preacher specifically about cover. Stones were cheapest, of course, but Reverend Meekhof had insisted that there was already enough gravel in the county and he'd always hated driving rural gravel roads. Tree bark would blow, especially on the edge of town, Foxhoven had warned, so they'd settled on molten rock. Molten, volcanic rock—probably seemed the right choice.

"You don't need me, I know," Meekhof said as he approached, pulling on his gloves, "but otherwise all I do is sit inside and watch talk shows."

"I don't need you yet," Foxhoven told him, pushing a wheelbarrow, his arms straining. "I'll let you know when."

"Don't patronize me either," the old preacher said. "You get ancient as I am and everybody talks to you as if you were a child or a fool." He straightened his shoulders for heavy lifting. "I couldn't think of a better hangout than right here on the front yard of my new house—all that wide prairie out there, the sun making me sweat," he said.

Foxhoven had to look up to be sure the preacher was overstating himself. "What I was thinking," he said, "was that once I get the plastic down," he pointed to the triangle, "you could smooth the cover." He flipped his thumb down at his cargo.

"You sound like my wife when I get too close to the kitchen," the preacher chuckled.

Foxhoven pulled the spade from where he'd jammed it into the stone bark and walked into the triangle to start on the biggest hole. Then he stabbed the ground ferociously.

Meekhof pulled off the gloves he'd just put on. "You know, for years I thought I was lazy—so did my parents. When I was a boy, the neighbor kids would take up some project—build a little car or something—and I'd stand around with my hands in my pockets, watching, scared to death of anything mechanical. You know how it is," he said. "Some kids seem to know by instinct where to find a choke. I never knew a thing. Still don't."

"You're a preacher," Duane said.

"Had to find a niche, and that's what I fell into," Meekhof told him.

Foxhoven stamped the blade into the soft dirt and started on the two-foot circle for the dogwood. Not once did he look at the old man.

"Nobody ever ends up exactly where they started," Meekhof said. "The fact is, when I was a kid I was terribly shy. It wasn't until I got to high school that I cut out trying to be like everybody else. I had a teacher who kept telling me that I couldn't hide my gifts under a bushel, and the only place for an educated man back then was the ministry, like my father. What did I know?"

"You sound like you wish you'd never done it," Foxhoven said, slipping off his shirt, then rolling it up and tossing it down on the brand-new driveway.

"No," Meekhof said, "I'm a lucky man. I look back on my years in the ministry and I don't regret much. Maybe I should have been a better father—seems the better I was at being a preacher, the worse a father I became. Something to that in every job, maybe. I don't know. What do you think?"

"People *love* you," Foxhoven said, working at that biggest hole.

"But the worst judge on earth is the one in here," Meekhof said, pointing at his chest. "My father used to say that you'll know what kind of a father you are once you see your grandkids."

Right there, a hole in the conversation opened wide enough for Duane Foxhoven to run a truck through. But he couldn't do it—somehow he just couldn't. He couldn't bring himself to expel the sweet bitterness that had lived in his heart for forty years. The handle of that spade slipped in his hands through the sweat. "Your grandkids have problems?" he said, hedging.

"Don't everybody's? Shoot, when you think about it, it was so much easier growing up when I was a kid. Church was everything—a place of worship and a place for fun—the only place in town. School wasn't fun, work wasn't fun—church was the whole works, community." He looked around quickly. "I'm going to get me a chair," he announced and walked up the driveway to the front of the garage, where three lawn chairs sat beneath the dining room window.

If Duane had looked up then, he would have seen the old man's one shoulder slouching slightly, his arms straining like a swimmer's do, cupping handfuls of air as he shuffled tediously uphill.

"You know, Margaret and I went to a concert the other night—maybe you heard about it—New Orleans Jazz Quartet or something like that," Meekhof said, hauling back a chair.

"Never heard of 'em," Foxhoven told him. Once he got down deep enough, he pulled the hose out and attached it to the spigot on the side of the house. Then he stood and filled the hole he'd dug.

"It was a few weeks ago now," Meekhof said, "but the whole time I was there watching those musicians, I told myself that the problem with people in Barneveld—and me too, I'm not scratching myself out on this one at all—is that somewhere along the line we never had ragtime."

Foxhoven put down the hose and ripped the plastic wrap away from the root ball.

"That music was some kind of joy, Foxhoven," the preacher said.

Duane likely shivered at the sound of his own name from the old preacher's mouth.

"Here you got four men who look like barbers, and one's got a soprano sax that makes a sound like something almost human. And there's a guy sitting beside the piano with a four-string banjo—big guy, arms like metwurst—and when he starts into 'The Old Rugged Cross,' he makes a sound like an angel's voice. The man playing the clarinet moves all over the place until the banjo takes the melody back, and the clarinet guy lays this tenor line down beneath like something you can lean on. And you know that pianist played entirely by heart? All night long he never looked at a page of music."

Meekhof said he never stopped talking, not for a second because he wanted to say something important.

"You know, when you're a kid and the piano teacher is always harping about not curving your wrist? Well, this guy kept his in a perfect curl because it's the only way he could make those fat hands of his dance over the keys the way he did. It was something."

The Foxhovens never had a piano. All they had were tires.

"But the miracle was that soprano sax. When he made that thing sing, when he brought the melody way up high, you could feel it in your chest—I swear it. I've heard pipe organs my whole life long that never moved me like that sax. You ever hear anything like that, Foxhoven?"

Duane Foxhoven kicked dirt into the cracks and tamped it with a blunt two-by-four, all the time feeling that who he was didn't matter one bit to this old man going on and on. All he knew was that he couldn't speak.

"That fat man playing the banjo had the face of a pumpkin and sometimes he'd just play, hunched over that thing so seriously. Then for no good reason, he'd break into a big smile as if he'd just told a joke," the preacher said. "They didn't play to the crowd at all—none of them did. They played to the music."

Duane wiped the sweat off his face with the back of his arm.

"It's crazy," the preacher said, "but I thought they were playing to the ghosts of ragtime, who likely had the seats in the front three rows—that's what I told my wife."

Duane scooped some black dirt on top of the root ball and smoothed it over, then made a little ridge to keep the water in when it had to be fed.

"Those guys had fun, you know?" Meekhof told him. "And the blessedness of it was the way they talked to each other, passed it around—you know what I'm saying? It was pure, selfless music—pure fun," the old preacher said. "In my life I learned how to preach, but not to give people room to do what they had to." That was part of what he wanted to say.

Duane never looked up.

Meekhof reached into his pocket and drew out his pipe nervously, then mouthed it, unlit. "I knew your father," he said. "I know who you are now. He used to be a member of my church, but he left when you were just a whippersnapper."

Foxhoven kept right on working. He tamped down the loose fill with the face of the hoe, then stepped lightly on the cracks until black water oozed from the edges.

"I can say it now—" Meekhof told him, "even if I couldn't back then. I wanted your father out of my church. I'm not proud of it either, in a way. If it makes any difference to you, Foxhoven, after so many years, I'm sorry."

The plans put three pygmy barberries along the foundation of the house. Duane eyeballed them where they sat, then walked over and put another foot or so between the middle one and the one closest to the front walk. He picked up the spade and traced a circle in the dirt and started into digging, then stepped back again. He backpedaled, stood beside the dogwood, and looked over the space at the foundation. And then he said, "You think three's enough here? They bloom dark violet, and they'll get maybe eighteen inches tall. I figured three was enough, and besides," he said, "I thought it was a holy number for a holy man."

"You got every right to be angry," Meekhof told him.

Foxhoven pushed the middle two barberries farther south and carried the little juniper into the corner close to the front porch. "This thing won't get high, but it'll spread out a ways," he said, circling an image with his hand. "If your wife wants to tend it, then maybe we ought to throw in a perennial bed on the other side of the walk here and leave it natural—no cover." He stepped toward the street and drew an oblong circle.

"To tell the truth," the preacher persisted, "I don't even remember what your dad looked like. We visited over there one night, and I was very young."

Foxhoven kicked the dirt off his shoes on the edge of the sidewalk.

"You get what I'm saying?" the preacher said.

Foxhoven spit, then pointed at the other side of the sidewalk. "You don't need me to put in a perennial bed here," he told him. "I'll just have one of the guys come by with a little fill, and if you come down to the shop, somebody'll help you pick out some things to throw in there." Then, for the first time, he looked at the preacher. "Perennials are popular nowadays," he said. "Lots of people want perennial beds. You can plant them so that something flowers just about every day of the summer."

The Reverend Meekhof stood up from the chair he'd dragged out there, circled it, and stood behind it—almost as if it were a pulpit. His hands shook. "I'm sorry," he said.

Foxhoven drew the back of his hand across his face to get the sweat out of his eyes. He took a deep breath, blew it out, and looked up into the sun. "I just hate it when it gets hot so early," he said angrily. Then he turned and picked up the spade.

Meekhof folded up his chair and walked back to the open garage.

Foxhoven jammed the spade into the soft fill, butted a cigarette out of the pack from his back pocket, and stuck one into the corner of his lips, then patted his chest fiercely to find the lighter that wasn't there.

That was the whole conversation. The old preacher said he felt terrible because nothing got through. When Reverend Meekhof told me that story, he had to fight back the tears.

The guys at the shop were surprised when the boss came back for coffee not a half hour later and told them to finish up at the Reverend Meekhof's place. "I got no time for it right now," he said angrily. "There's just too much to do around here."

This year that dogwood towers over the front porch of the Meekhofs' retirement home on the east edge of town, a place that still faces farmland because no one has yet built a house across the street, although people say it's only a matter of time. The Meekhofs don't live there anymore. Three years ago already, the Reverend had been napping lightly in an easy chair in the family room, his eyes closed, listening with one ear to the local news on the little color TV set he and his wife had bought to sit on the kitchen counter.

His wife of all those years had been making spaghetti, trying to get the pasta right, a new recipe, when she glanced up at her husband and saw his face turned sharply to the side—just a glance was all she needed to know immediately that he was gone. It was so easy, she said, that sometimes she thought it was just like with Enoch in the Bible—her husband just walked away with the Lord.

The Reverend Cecil Meekhof was one of those people who really shouldn't have missed his own funeral. He always could work a crowd like a master politician, and he would have loved to see his old church so full of people that they had to stand behind the glass in the fellowship hall just to be a part of the funeral everybody saw as a celebration of one wonderful life.

Sarah Esselink played the piano, and she pounded out tunes that probably came as close to ragtime as anything heard in Meekhof's church.

Some stores in town shut down for the afternoon, almost like Good Friday. The *News* covered the whole front page with a series of stories about the life of a man who came to be so deeply associated with the town that sometimes even the Congregationalists and Baptists would refer to him as "the bishop of Barneveld."

Duane Foxhoven didn't attend. He was at the interment, where literally hundreds of mourners stood around the little tent sheltering the casket from the hot sun. The preacher's family—including their own children—listened to one of the grandsons, recently ordained, read very slowly through a psalm. Mrs. Meekhof, people said later, mouthed the words as her grandson read, not to show the world she knew the passage, but in a way that made people think she was, like a grandma, coaxing her husband's most obvious heir to make sure he got it out just right.

Duane Foxhoven was there in his work clothes because it's been his job for almost twenty years to put down the deceased once the crowd leaves the cemetery for the coffee and cake back at church. It's a job he inherited from his father, since Brush had the first implement capable of digging grave sites from the thick clay, heavy as pottery, beneath a foot or so of rich Iowa topsoil. The job is a natural fit for a man in Duane's profession since he keeps the grass cut out there anyway, the weeds down, the whole place—even the flower garden up near the street—dignified and maintained. Duane Foxhoven knows very well how to keep things in their place.

He was standing beside his truck in the parking lot, along with two guys from his crew and his son, Scott, who I think is starting to find himself. All of them were smoking as the crowd began to disperse, a crowd so huge that its very size must have turned Duane's insides into a tight fist. Later, when people were gone but the tent over the casket was still there, he told the guys it was a job he wanted to do himself—put the old man into the ground, a gesture even his son read as something borne from respect.

Now Duane might have also buried something of himself at that moment, but what was in him was already too heavy and maybe too deep to be resurrected—except by the power of someone outside himself, a power he shucked long ago for reasons so complicated and yet so simple that they make this whole story horribly understandable. All he buried that day in that gleaming casket was the body of the Reverend Cecil Meekhof—not the good Reverend's soul and certainly not his own scrapbook of memories.

Other than Memorial Day, when the place is decorated in fresh, red geraniums and new American flags, and other than the days when funeral processions wind their way through the gravestones, no one spends much time in the Barneveld graveyard. Occasionally, Duane sends somebody from his crew over to cut the grass, but often as not he does it himself, sometime toward nightfall, when he doesn't care to be at home, which is quite often.

Sometimes when he's at the cemetery, the wide prairie skies to the west are streaked with colors that are absolutely heavenly, at play with beauty. He'd see it if he'd ever stop to look and blur his eyes the way he might have at that Christmas tree so long ago—the way I imagine him doing, just slightly out of focus, like so many of us do as children.

Once a year in late spring, almost like a ritual, Duane takes a half-pint of red paint along when he cuts the grass with that big green John Deere mower. Sometimes toward the edge of night when he can just make out the line of where he's going, he stops, takes that half-pint out of his jacket pocket, and with what must be a kind of sweet unearthly delight, pours it like blood over the square granite monument set over the remains of the bishop of Barneveld.

Every year, a couple of days pass. Maybe someone reports seeing that stain out there, maybe not. If no one does, he reports the vandalism himself—claims he discovered it when he was cutting grass. Regularly, the cops tell the family, almost as if it were a warning about something portentous. Otherwise, they don't tell a soul. What for? Why blot the good man's memory now that he's gone? Why send all of Barneveld into a swoon over the way kids nowadays show no respect? The only person who'd profit from anyone's knowing, the police claim, is the jerk who does it. He's the one looking to be known.

The police have asked Foxhoven to try to catch the guy because it's happened every year. But Duane shakes his head and tells them he'd rather not spend a night out there in the graveyard, and anyway all it takes to clean up that stone is a little hot water since whoever does it is kind enough to use latex. All he says is that he wonders sometimes what kind of grudge this nut must carry.

"Against the Reverend Meekhof?" the cops say.

"Who knows what might have happened?" Foxhoven says.

He leaves the red splash out there for a few days, telling those who care that he doesn't have the time, just like that, to run out and scrub it up. Time is money, after all; he'll get to it when he can.

And he does. Three days, at most, he figures. Let it sit there a little while. He might even tell himself that three days sounds biblical.

I know he's the guilty party because his son, Scott, told me. He saw his father do it once a couple of years ago. Like I said, Scott may be coming around. The fact that he told me is no small thing.

I've not told anyone because in some ways what Duane does once a year hurts no one but himself. In the times I've tried to be nice to him, I've never gotten any further than Reverend Meekhof did that day on his new front lawn.

Undoubtedly, there's some pleasure for Duane in the act, or he wouldn't do it. Maybe some day he'll stop, enough red paint having been spilled.

It happened again this year.

So I pray for Laurie, who doesn't know—and shouldn't, I suppose—and whose story of perseverance could never be told in any church, even though lots of folks know its sharp and hurtful edges. And I pray for Scott, who is now the third generation in a legacy of sin and stubbornness. Forty years of desert wandering is what the Lord gave the disobedient Israelites—one whole generation. But Scott is already the third generation in a series of victims of whatever sin it was that occurred just inside the door of Brush Foxhoven's home.

And, as hard as it is, I pray too for Duane, the obdurate— a man who needs so badly to know in his soul that once long ago divine blood was spilled over the graves of all who confess and believe. Lord knows he's got a way to go.

The Temptations of Sarah Esselink

To see Sarah Esselink outfitted in a Santa suit would be to behold Saint Nick himself. She has his round face, his pudgy nose, and his apple cheeks. What's more, her sticklike legs seem inadequate to lug her heft around town. She has his eyes too—bright, sparkling twinkles that glitter when she's at the piano—and everyone recognizes that silly, chattering giggle of hers, even in a crowd.

Calvary Church has its share of guilt-ridden folks with overcast faces, but no one would accuse Sarah Esselink of being among them—even though, given what her son's become, many would say she has a right to be dour.

She has never led any of the many organizations she's served—Ladies' Guild, Booster Club, Legion Auxiliary—but most people would say Sarah long ago found her own distinguished place on the piano bench at Calvary. She was blessed with massive hands, a titanic heart, and sensitivities so promiscuous that whenever she hears children sing the old favorite hymns—"The Old Rugged Cross" or "I Come to the Garden Alone"—those thick fingers of hers wiggle into her purse for the tatted hanky.

Such powerful hands and such a tender heart make her piano playing remarkable. She is self-made as a pianist, having pulled up her skills from the bootstraps of her own meager talents; she hears a melody once and owns it thereafter, as if God in his infinite wisdom stowed a computer chip in that round head of hers.

Everything she plays is a copy, but nothing sounds quite the same when Sarah lays hold of it. Everything she hammers out seems vaudevillian. To her, every line of music stands in need of grace. She can lace together a piece like "Beautiful Savior" with five minutes of leap-frogging arpeggios. Luther's "A Mighty Fortress" comes out resembling the Taj Mahal. She once finished the "Hallelujah Chorus" with a gash of lightning struck over the keys with the back of her thumbnail—an event so memorable that some members remember that Sunday as effortlessly as they do the assassination of JFK.

But on the sly, this wonderful woman has been addicted to supermarket tabloids for more than twenty years. She doesn't buy her copies of the *Enquirer* at Foodland in town, where she's likely to be seen; she refuses a subscription, although her husband, Eldon, has asked about it often as a birthday gift. Investing that heavily would be like making a commitment to sin, she reasoned. Instead, she simply grabs them from the racks of out-of-town stores in acts of what she considers insane passion, reads them, and then destroys them at home. She does not put them out front for recycling, where some garbage man might find them and look up suspiciously at the Esselink house.

She and Eldon, a man so silent and dignified you might think him Navajo, live in an old house with three stories on the west edge of town. Although the loads of laundry have shrunk considerably since the kids left home, some time ago Sarah began to notice that after lugging the upstairs hamper down into the basement, she was able to do little but wheeze. Her fatigue was undeniable.

"You'd better check it out," Eldon told her.

She's convinced, however, that she goes too often to the doctor already. "He'll just say I'm overweight," she told her husband. "I know what'll happen. I'll go in and he'll have me undress, and he'll say it's time for me to diet. 'Lose forty pounds,' he'll say, 'next patient.' You want to live with me then?"

Eldon long ago learned to live with his good wife, so he let her alone.

Nothing keeps Sarah away from her piano. When she plays at home, she keeps a hymnal on the rack in front of her, not so much to follow the music as to remind her of her options. She'll barrel through a favorite, then fan the pages until she falls on a title she hasn't had a shot at in a while. Her arms have considerable girth, her wrists are thick, and her hands— barely wide enough to span an octave—have the heft of sandbags. She plays prodigiously.

A few months ago, after playing only two verses of "Trust and Obey," Sarah had to drop her arms. She could barely hold her hands up. She felt almost as if she would collapse. She had to go to Doc Howells.

"It's lucky you did," he told her when she came in yet that afternoon. "I'm going to put you in the hospital in Sioux City, but first we have to run a few tests. Call Eldon and tell him. It's not an emergency, but I'm not letting you out of here."

"How can you say it's not an emergency if I'm staying here?" Sarah demanded.

"It's *not* an emergency," the doctor repeated. "It's something we can take care of without really complicated surgery— but something we should take care of right away. You're all plugged up probably," he told her, his hand on her shoulder. "We got to flush your arteries."

She turned away quickly and saw a picture of a human carcass—neither man nor woman—pinned to the wall, all the muscles exposed.

"I'll call and get you in," Dr. Howells told her. "Now don't get upset. The treatment isn't at all what it would have been fifteen years ago. We'll run some tests, but I think I know the problem."

"What is it?" she asked.

"I'll wait till Eldon gets here," he said. "Then I'll explain it to both of you. Don't worry," he told her again, and then he kissed her on the temple—the kiss of Judas is what she thought it was.

She didn't call Eldon right away because he was working somewhere—he's a master plumber. Besides, she thought immediately of her son Carl, who's not her son with the problem. He may be *a* problem, but he's not *the* problem. Carl is a doctor in Omaha, one of those who only keeps office hours—very rich, just treats allergies. Divorced, but scads of money, she claims.

"He told me he was going to flush me out," she told Carl when she got him on the phone. She had pulled his number from a card in her purse and reversed the charges to his office.

"That's all he told you?" Carl asked.

"He said he was going to wait for your father to get here and then explain the whole thing before shipping me off to Sioux City. I'm supposed to go to the hospital right away." She looked up at the door because she didn't want the nurse coming in to hear her on the phone to her son and not to Eldon.

"I'll drive up," Carl said. "I don't trust GPs."

Unfortunately, his dropping everything only made things worse. If her own son wasn't going to say anything over the phone and the doctor wanted to explain the whole operation only after Eldon was there, how could anyone expect her *not* to worry, Sarah thought. Besides, just a bit later, she failed the treadmill test miserably.

"What happens," Dr. Howells told them when Eldon finally showed up in his coveralls, "is that you get crud in your arteries." He looked at Eldon. "Like old pipes."

Eldon nodded.

"What we've got to do is go in there and clean up a little. Put a little Drano in."

They both knew he was trying to make a joke.

"Actually, it's a balloon is all it is," he told them. "We push a little balloon in there and blow it up a little, and push back the crud so that your blood flows more easily. It's really quite simple," he said. "You can't believe how easy it is."

"Where does the balloon go?" Sarah asked.

The doctor pointed at the very center of his being.

"I called Carl," Sarah told Eldon when the two of them were driving to Sioux City. "He said he was coming. He's on his way."

Eldon nodded.

"You suppose we ought to call Mary?"

"I already did," he told her. "She's coming too."

Mary is a social worker in Elgin, Illinois.

"It's really nothing at all," Sarah said.

The fact is, Sarah had always thought she'd die long before Eldon, despite the odds of men going first. She says she had always thought her weight would take her, making her the exception to the rule and thereby sending Eldon into the arms of some good-looking widow who could cook.

"I'm supposed to play at church this week," she told Eldon. "Maybe you better call the pastor and get him to line somebody else up."

"It's Tuesday," Eldon said. "By Sunday, everything will be perfectly fine."

She rolled her eyes. "Don't be playing games, Eldon. Call the pastor—just call him." That's when I got involved.

When I visited Sarah, she was checked in, fourth floor, the big window east giving her a nice view of the stockyards. She told me that she had fiddled with the remote until she figured out how to get something on TV, but nothing on the screen really went into her head because just then, right after she had arrived, she couldn't think about anything but the fact that it was her heart they were talking about here—not a gall bladder or a stiff cough.

Carl, her doctor son, was coming—and you know he must have patients who are steaming mad, what with him canceling appointments the way he must have. Some of those patients were anxious too, she figured, probably really needing to see him—wheezing hard themselves, she thought. Why would Carl come if it really was nothing at all? He probably told his nurse that he had to cancel all his appointments, that he had to go home. "It's an *emergency*"—that's probably the exact word he used.

And Mary was coming, all the way from Illinois. Mary would come alone, and oh, my, that would leave Frank with the kids in Illinois. He'd have to cook and get them off to school and whatnot. Maybe they'd just go out for meals. That'd be better, of course—and the kids would love it. Mary certainly wouldn't take the kids along—they should be in school. Of course she wouldn't take the kids along, but then she shouldn't really leave them alone with Frank either. All on account of her heart. Oh, what a mess. That's what Sarah was thinking.

And had anyone called Chris?

Chris, you may have guessed, is *the problem*. He lives in Los Angeles, and he's single. For years, Sarah has believed that his problem was little more than not being able to find the right gal. That's still what she likes to think. It's what she tells people when they ask about Chris—which they haven't done now for about three years. People in this town aren't dumb, at least not when it comes to smelling scandals.

Chris is gay, and everyone who understands life in the late twentieth century knows it, or thinks they do. Because he is single and lives in California, because he wears his thinning hair cut very short, and because those who remember Chris Esselink from high school will never forget his strange drawings, they all think they know the truth.

No one says it—at least not to Sarah or Eldon. Most people

in Barneveld are quite comfortable with that kind of arrangement—knowing everything, saying very little. It's pretty much a way of life. The only effect Chris Esselink's being a homosexual has made on life in his hometown is a bit of restraint. He occasionally prompts some wife to elbow her husband at a Bible study when he starts into gay-bashing—*if*, of course, the Esselinks happen to be in the Bible study. Otherwise, it's open season, especially in an election year.

No one in Barneveld really knows, except Eldon the Silent and Sarah—Chris's mom and dad. They know because their son, Christiaan, told them straightforwardly three years ago, via a letter. It included a long explanation, a defense, and an assurance—something booklike Sarah read maybe six times a day the first week after it arrived, then sealed up with Scotch tape and stuck away forever.

Of course, they showed no one, not even Chris's older siblings, both of whom knew anyway from a copy of the same letter addressed to each of them. But no one at Calvary Church knows for sure, even though they all suspect the truth.

"I called Chris," Mary told her parents when she came later, alone. "I wanted him to know."

For a moment, conversation stopped abruptly.

"Anyway, it's no big deal," Sarah announced. "Lots of people have this little operation. I don't know why everybody has to be here."

"Is he coming?" Eldon asked.

"He was going to try," Mary replied.

"I don't know what all the fuss is about," Sarah insisted.

"The fuss is you're our mother," Mary told her. "Would you stop griping and let us love you for a minute here?"

"It's not that I'm going to die," she said.

"That's a *good* reason for us to come," Mary said. "Better than the other."

She'd had a hold of her mother's hand ever since she'd come into the room, and after a while, Sarah thought that Mary's being there on the bed the way she was got a little close. All it did was make her more scared.

"And who's taking care of my grandchildren?" she asked her daughter.

"Frank's a veteran, Mom," Mary said. "I've been working full-time for years. He's a better cook than I am."

Still, Sarah thought, there was too much fuss over an operation that everyone—even Carl, her big-time doctor son—said was nothing to be alarmed about.

That evening in the Sioux City hospital, when the kids stepped out with Eldon to get something to eat, Sarah had a moment alone. She told me she tried to think it all through—what should actually happen, since the operation, as everyone said, really wasn't that big of a deal. She'd have to tell Carl and Mary that it wasn't necessary for them to hang around the hospital all day—there was nothing they could do anyway. Magazines would get old inside of an hour. She'd tell them to stay back in Barneveld, an hour north, until she was out of the surgery. Mary still has some old friends in town, Sarah thought—every five years Donna Mills asks if Mary's coming to the high school reunion, and Sherrie Rademaker would also love a visit, especially after her last baby had come so unexpectedly. Carl should really have a tour of the new clinic in town, or else he could stop in at Frenchie Schoon's, since Frenchie was in the office now anyway, having built up that welding business to the point where all he did was shuffle paper.

Chris. There really were no old friends, no place where he could talk shop. He was an accountant, but she wouldn't think of sending him to Herm Felton's office, where every wall had some big game trophy head. Chris was the problem.

What could she suggest for him, after all? Maybe he could cook. She could bring that up—suggest Chris cook for the others because he sometimes wrote about the fun he was having learning how to make this and that and other foreign-language stuff.

She couldn't forget Chris really. They'd named him "Christiaan," after his grandfather, the mason—but he didn't inherit his grandfather's shoulders. Just a year before, the *Star* had run something about a San Francisco parade in an issue Sarah didn't buy because she didn't want to see the pictures inside.

She told me she got to thinking about Chris really seriously that night when she was alone with her heart problems. She said how happy she was that he'd never written to tell them how much he despised his parents. Her worst nightmare was that someday he would blame them for the way he was, the way all of those people do on talk shows, everybody with problems. How many times don't you see, nowadays, parents and kids having it out in front of millions of viewers?

It was something they'd never talked about, of course. Eldon never said much, and she'd always blamed herself anyway. After all, she'd read about pushy mothers and heard it often enough on television to know that theory inside and out. She'd read about faults she knew she had—lots of them too—and sometimes she wondered how it was that the Lord didn't give you the ability to see yourself the way your kids did. She'd always tried to do what was right; she'd never flinched on that. Her father, a mason, had molded a code of right and wrong so readable he might have fashioned the Ten Commandments himself on a cement slate if Moses hadn't beat him to it. She'd just followed her father's lead.

What she focused on constantly—more than what kind of thing Chris was doing with other men (she couldn't bring herself to think about that), more than AIDS—was his soul. How could he do what he did—what she thought he did—if he still had faith? Even if, like he said, there was only one man . . . she couldn't bring herself to use the words even in her mind.

If what Chris had become was somehow her fault, she thought that night before the operation, then it was only fair that she know where that fault lay. But the only thing she'd ever come up with really—there were other things too, of course, like harping at Eldon sometimes for not doing the little jobs around the house he spent all week long doing for other people—but the only real problem she could find in her life, aside from a little too much afternoon television, was those magazines. That's what she told me, the preacher, the night before the operation on her heart.

"Why do you read those things? They're garbage!" her daughter had told her years ago already, when Mary was in college. After that, when Mary had come home, Sarah hid them downstairs between the stacks of old newspapers.

And there was the night all the kids came home for Eldon's sixtieth birthday—all that laughing and joking, and all of a sudden, out of nowhere, Chris said, "It took me ten years to forgive you for reading that stuff." He said it absolutely in stitches—as if it were meant to be funny. "I mean, the whole time we were growing up, I thought everybody in town had them at home. And then Thompson—the only teacher in high school I respected—just gagged on the *Enquirer,*" he said, wiping tears from his eyes. "I was so embarrassed, Mother!" he said, laughing hard. "You don't still read them—do you?"

She said at that moment she could do nothing but drop her eyes.

"Mom!" Mary exclaimed. "Tell us you don't."

"Mom's got a right to her kicks!" Carl said, and all three of them burst into laughter, even Eldon, who brought an arm down from where he'd had it across his chest and laid his hand, like a father might have, across his wife's wrists to help her bear her burdens.

66

Besides, Sarah reasoned that night in the hospital, some things in those magazines people needed to know—about breast surgery, for instance, and information about the president.

Was it so wrong?

But what if I die tomorrow? That's what she told me she was thinking. What if that thing gets poked up too far and then pops like a birthday balloon right there in my heart?

Major surgery—even if it was only a balloon in a clogged artery—had a way of focusing Sarah Esselink's life as sharply as a date at dawn with the gallows.

There she lay, in a hospital bed forty miles from her piano room, remembering what her baby boy had said about it taking ten years for him to forgive her. Right there in front of me, she broke into prayer. She went before the Lord in her hospital gown, the night before a thin little balloon would be thrust up through a vein in her leg toward something clogged, an operation thousands have gone through without so much pain as that from a hangnail.

"Father in heaven," she said, "I need to live through this one. If you let me live," she told the Lord, "I'll be your faithful servant. I'll give them up too," she promised. "I will."

She didn't name the sin because she knew the Lord was fully capable of filling in blanks. She lay there and cut a deal with God—his healing hand for her abstinence. When that prayer was over, she looked up at me with some peace on her face. Later, she said, after I'd left, she felt the Lord's hand comforting her gingerly just before Chris finally called.

Maybe it was unfortunate, maybe not, but Chris couldn't make it home—he called her to tell her so. "It's really nothing, Mother," he told her. He was the only one of her kids who insisted on calling her "Mother." "Countless people have undergone this thing and come out ready to play tennis."

"I'm only worried about the piano," she told him.

"You can't keep a good woman down," her son said.

She was full of the burden, so she found it hard to be polite.

"How's everything else?" he inquired.

There was nothing else.

"What do you mean?" she said.

"I'm just making conversation, Mother," he told her.

She didn't know what to say to him. There she sat in her bed, holding the phone, full to the ears with what she wanted to ask him.

"How's work?" she said finally.

"You're worried, aren't you? It's not like you not to jabber."

"If it wouldn't be around my heart—if it would only be my kidneys or something. You know, you've got an extra one of those." Even as she said it, she knew he was the only one who got the whole truth from her. Everyone else saw only her strength.

"You're going to be all right," he told her.

"You pray for me, you hear?" she said.

"I'll pray."

"You pray much, Chris?" she asked.

"I pray," he said.

"Much?"

"I didn't think God kept a tally," he told her.

"The Bible says 'pray without ceasing,'" she told him. "It's in there."

"Look, Mother," he said. "I just called to reassure you, you know? I don't want to get into anything here."

"I'm your mother," she said.

"I'm not arguing that," he said.

And that's when it finally came out.

"Christiaan," she said, "was it something I didn't do right or something? Tell me if it was. I need to know. I'm facing the knife tomorrow." The silence spread out so long that she wondered if her boy had simply hung up the phone. "Chris?" she said again.

But he still didn't speak.

"Chris—are you still there?"

"The question implies, Mother," he said, "that my life is somehow screwed up."

"You want me to believe that it isn't?"

"I understand you, Mom," he said.

"I don't want to stand before the Lord with things not right between you and me," she told him shakily, her nerves now tightening in her throat. Her voice squeaked. "If it's something I did, then I want to know because tonight I want to be forgiven."

All of us keep a running score of parental transgressions, transgressions likely better forgotten, so it's possible he started thumbing through the memories himself. But to his credit, he never started into the list—if there was one. Perhaps he was thinking only that his mother didn't really need a sleepless night.

"Whatever sins you carry up to judgment, Mother," he said, "you know as well as I do that your Lord Jesus will take them away. I've never questioned my mother's faith."

"Is he *your* Lord too?" she asked earnestly.

I'm sure that Chris Esselink knew this much, having grown up with Eldon and Sarah: He knew what kind of answer would bring her rest. "He is," Christiaan said. That's all.

Whether he meant it or not, or even how he meant it, he didn't explain to her. But on the night before she faced some serious tinkering with the pound of muscle that animates her entire being, Sarah Esselink wanted only to hear the words he'd just told her. With that, she could go through whatever tomorrow held.

For hundreds of years, Christians have painted heavenly glory as if it were a monstrous Mormon Tabernacle Choir in the "Up Yonder Metrodome," a trillion voices singing praises to the glory of the Lord. Today, some Christians find such an image to be out of touch with the media generation. But that night, once she put the phone down, Sarah Esselink went to sleep with visions of that very monstrous choir and she herself at the bench of a crystalline baby grand, accompanying the whole world of saints, even if Christiaan wasn't among those assembled in the loft.

All the anxiety about the operation turned out to be unnecessary. Medical science has just about perfected that delicate little surgical operation, and the next morning, without much fuss at all, Sarah's heavy-laden arteries opened up like tulips in soft April sunshine.

Despite the fact that the whole operation was a resounding success, Sarah Esselink held tenaciously to her deathbed commitment. Once out of the hospital, she didn't buy another supermarket tabloid. She scrambled for the shortest lines at the stores, and when she got stuck behind two or three other customers, she picked out mouth spray or extra batteries from the junk that's always kept right up there at the checkout, just to keep her eyes off the headlines of the *Star* or the *Enquirer*. Just being around those tabloids made her nervous and irritated. Often enough, she hauled Eldon along to do some serious shopping because she didn't trust herself. He claims her health picked up and her energy increased, but sometimes he wondered if she wasn't more troubled even with her arteries as clean as new plastic conduits.

She never lost the urge—she just sat on it. In the four months that passed since her operation, not once did she so much as pick up one of those magazines while waiting in line.

You've got to love Sarah Esselink. She thought she could carry out her end of the bargain she'd taken out with the Lord's will, that she could pull it off once her heart was running smoothly.

Then came Florida.

Sarah said Eldon didn't like the grass down there because it is not really made for walking, only for show. It's thick and wiry and almost cactuslike. All it's meant for, Eldon told her, was to look green. And the bugs, Eldon complained, there were tons of bugs. A person could make a real living in pest control. That's what he told Sarah, not Al and Betty Verdoorn, in whose trailer they stayed for a week.

"You don't like it, hon?" Sarah asked him.

"I didn't say I don't like it," he told her. "It's just not like home."

"You'd be freezing your buns off," she told him. "If you were back home, you'd be dressed in two coveralls. You saw the weather last night—two below."

"All I said was they got bug problems down here—that and I don't care to walk on the sharp grass," Eldon said.

They were sitting out in a pair of bright yellow lounge chairs lined up with another half-dozen along a shuffleboard court where Al and another guy were doing battle. From somewhere neither of them could identify, a warm breeze picked up a smell so delicious it almost seemed sinful. The fact was, Sarah loved Florida, even thought about bringing up the possibility of them buying their own mobile home, but figured it would be smarter for her to nudge it into the conversation when they got back to Iowa.

"I never thought I'd see you enjoy shuffleboard," she told him.

"When in Rome," Eldon said. At least he liked something.

Betty came out with a tray full of steaming cups of tea, which was nice. She offered them each one, then sat on a lounge beside Sarah, who still couldn't get over the fact that all of those old women wore shorts all the time.

"I was thinking," Betty said, holding her cup up to her lips. "They got the nation's biggest Christmas tree over in Boca. They ship it in all the way from Oregon or somewhere. They

71

take it all apart up there, label the pieces, and then assemble it down here. It's a white spruce or something—Al would know what kind. We ought to go over there—it's really something to see," Betty said.

"World's biggest Christmas tree?" Sarah said. "Bigger than the one at the White House?"

"That's what they say."

And so they went to see it. Sarah told me it's huge. She said the only thing taller on the flat coastal landscape is the endless range of high-rise condos along the beach. Sarah claims that monstrous tree towers above the suburban world like a New England lighthouse.

The closer you get to the spot where it stands, the higher the parking rate, Sarah said, but Al knew exactly where to leave the car, having hauled just about every snowbird from Barneveld they'd hosted in the last few years to one of this tree's predecessors. He found a spot about six blocks away on a street full of little frame bungalows, each with its own wire fence.

"Bad neighborhood?" Eldon asked when Al was locking up the Dodge.

"It's *all* bad down here," Al said. "There's crime down here that's worse almost than anywhere—even Washington, D.C. Somebody's always getting murdered—every day."

Sarah said she put a hand in the crook of Eldon's arm. "People don't keep their yards up either, do they?" she observed.

The sun was wonderfully gentle, almost out of sight to the west, but you could still see that the place was a mess. Shards of palm trees were lying all over the sidewalk, and that wild grass Eldon complained about grew out of control like wiry, unruly hair. Broken-down motorcycles stood ghostlike in the yards, and trash littered the weeds along the street, enough nickels in empty cans to make a living, Eldon told her. Wasn't at all like Barneveld. This place needed a thorough going-over.

But whenever she looked up at that tall Christmas tree, Sarah thought about what kind of testimony that tree was in this run-down neighborhood, a towering Christmas tree like that, reminding everyone that it really was Christmas down here, a holiday celebrating the coming of the Lord Jesus, whom everyone, it seemed, could forget about so easily nowadays.

"Is it some church that puts it up?" she asked.

"You wait," Betty said. "They got a whole bunch of displays set up for Christmas. You won't believe all the lights."

"What church can afford to pay the bill?" Eldon said.

"There's big churches down here," Al told him. "You can't believe the size of the churches. They're huge—thousands of people, as many as in all of Holland County."

The big tree stood in a kind of park, and even in the fading daylight, just to see it was a thrill, Sarah told me. Along with the others, they pushed forward slowly, some of them with blankets as if they were going to sit for fireworks.

When the kids were little, Eldon and Sarah used to take them to Sioux City on the Friday before Christmas, when Younkers would open up their specially decorated holiday display windows downtown. Everybody would be there, no matter how cold it was. But what she found around that huge assembled tree was a display of Christmas ornaments like she'd never seen—millions of lights hung from trees and strung around animated productions of Santa and his elves busy in their Christmas workshop, Rudolf polishing his nose, and Mickey Mouse and Minnie getting everything ready for Christmas Eve. Everywhere you looked there was silver light, like a sky suddenly gone mad with stars. Sarah said she would have loved to share the spectacle with the grandkids. "Wouldn't they just love this, Eldon?" she said.

It would be wonderful to see all the children, Sarah thought, their bright eyes dancing with all the magic. She had to stop herself from just breaking down and crying—that's exactly how warm it made her feel in her spacious, newly repaired heart. A whole city park full of storefront displays, all of them circling around this huge tree decorated with ropes of ribbon and ornaments of all colors, big and round as basketballs.

"You get up close and you can see what they did," Eldon said when he found her back at the manger display. "Every limb's got a number. It's like an artificial tree, really," he told her, shaking his head.

"Then don't look so close," she told him. "Just sit back here and don't always look for the worst in things." She turned to Betty. "Who pays for all of this?" she asked.

"The office of that newspaper," Betty said. "There's an office over there. They write that newspaper—what's its name, Al?"

I've tried to write this story just as Sarah told me, and in doing so I've set you up for the same kind of cheap trick she set me up for. But she did it for a reason, because Sarah herself nearly collapsed when Al, without batting an eye, without a hint of malice or sarcasm, with nothing at all to indicate any sense of Sarah's own shock, said, "The *Enquirer* pays for all of this. Their office is right over there."

"You know," Betty said, "that awful magazine you see in stores—it looks like a newspaper, but it's got all that stupid stuff in it?"

"Sure," Eldon said, covering for his wife, "I know that one."

Sarah heard the words like a message from the soul of the cosmos. She stood amid the glow of holiday lights, stunned. She knew, unequivocally, that the Lord works in mysterious ways, and she recognized something of his voice in the name of the newspaper, even if she wasn't at all sure of what her Lord meant to present her with just then.

"The office is right around the corner there," Al said. "They give tours."

When Sarah told me all of this, she demurred from expressing the desire I know flashed through her system. I know that's true, but I also know she wouldn't have told me. Barneveld people don't say much about desire, *period*—not only because some of their desires are occasionally unseemly, but also because desire itself is more than a little suspect. What likely exploded in her was a passion she'd effectively repressed for four months, poor thing. To say that she wanted that tour would be an understatement with the proportions of that huge Northwest spruce. Of course she wanted to go.

"We went on the tour once," Betty said. "It's very interesting. Want to?"

It's not every day that Sarah Esselink is at a loss for words.

"Maybe we ought to go in," Eldon said, just for her.

The three of them stood there in silence, waiting for some sign from Sarah.

"You want to go?" Eldon asked her. "You know what kind of paper they're talking about?" Then he looked at her, as if expecting a certain answer, smiling as if to let her know he thought it was all right.

"Sure," she said.

And this is how she thought it through, lightning fast: God wouldn't have brought them here if he didn't think it was just fine for her to take that tour. And besides, wasn't it incredible that a magazine like that could bring so much warmth to the faces of all those children here for the holidays? Above all the refuse on the street stood a magnificent Christmas tree, the only giant spruce in all of Southern Florida. Behind every dark cloud there's sure enough some kind of a silver lining, she told herself.

Just then someone threw the switch on that big tree, the Florida sun having fallen from the western sky. But Sarah couldn't look up and gaze in amazement the way all the others did, the hundreds of people who stared at the sudden explosion of lights over a part of the city with bad grass and no upkeep, even bugs. She took one quick glance, but that's all. She didn't even really see what she was looking at because

75

what was in her eyes made her reach in her purse for that tatted handkerchief. That's how beautiful it was, and to think that it was that old newspaper that did it, she thought—that was something.

"You want to go on that tour?" asked Eldon the Silent one more time once the oohing and aahing had ceased.

"Sure," she said. So they did. They took the tour. They faced the beast.

Not long ago, I took Eldon out for coffee, and we went through the whole story of his wife's heart and the trip to Florida. I heard about that huge Christmas tree again from him, just to be sure the story she'd told me was accurate.

I asked about the magazines, and Eldon laughed because he'd never really considered her interest in those things as much of a sin as she did herself.

This is what he told me: When Sarah got back to Barneveld, she kept up her abstinence for a while, then bought one *Star* somewhere out of town on a weekend. That was the beginning. She's not in over her head, Eldon told me, smiling, but she'll pick up something once in a while. He lets it go because he's happier himself, he claims, what with his wife of all those years not pulled tight as a machine wire.

Nobody in Barneveld knows all of this, of course, and even if they did they wouldn't think it as important as it was to Sarah Esselink—that much ado about an operation that really isn't much of a bother to anyone. Nobody even guesses anything traumatic occurred through that hospital stay and the tinkering the doctors did with Sarah's heart. Nobody guesses anything because nothing that happened changed a note in the way Sarah bangs the church piano. She still offers every last hymn in streamers and bows over shiny holiday paper, Fanny Crosby in rococo. Every anthem ends with a thirty-second bass chord salutation chasing madly down the keyboard.

To my mind, she's healthy in body and soul, not so comfortable with her own sin, but at least not a victim of her own precious guilt. Some summer night, if you walk by her house, you'll hear more energy from those keys than you could imagine a woman with her years and burdens could ever raise. Maybe her playing is a bit overdone. There are some in Calvary Church who think so.

But when Sarah Esselink willfully broke the deal she'd cut with the Lord one harried night in the Sioux City hospital, she pulled something new out of the strictures of her own faith. Now she talks to her son Christiaan a bit more regularly on the phone, Eldon says, calls him just to talk and doesn't reverse the charges, even though he's a whole lot richer than they are.

And even though she's passionately interested in her son— as she is in all three kids—Eldon says she's stopped fighting him now. Somehow, oddly enough, it took the *Enquirer* to teach her the lesson she's heard a thousand times on Sunday mornings—to be still and trust the Lord.

Mindy Brink at River Bend

Almost two months after the accident that crippled Lenny Bolstad and made Mindy Brink the closest thing all of Barneveld had ever seen to Mother Teresa, I met her brother Alan, her twin, on the sidewalk outside the drugstore. Alan is quiet, like his sister, not given to happy faces or public displays of any particular emotion. He smiled as we met, but then I turned and called out his name because I hadn't really spoken to him since the accident—not by himself anyway. I had talked with his family, yes, but he and Mindy were already old enough to have their own lives.

I asked him how it was going. He brought his lips up and nodded, in the stoic manner Barneveld breeds into its own—as if to say there's no reason anyone should be concerned. Long ago I learned to look past that public face, so I disposed of the amenities, walked up to him, and said, "What are you telling her?"

Immediately, he dropped his eyes.

"She's your sister, your twin," I said, not accusingly. "What do you tell her?"

He shook his head in a way I read as defeated.

"What exactly happened?" I asked. "Do you ever talk about it?"

And then he looked at me as if on that point there were no questions.

"Do you know?" I pressed on.

He shrugged his shoulders.

"She doesn't have to give him everything," I told him. "You know that, don't you?"

He nodded.

"Do you try to tell her that?" I asked him.

He looked up at me. "What she does is what she wants to do," he said, and then he looked around at Main Street as if to catch some sly photographer recording all of this on film. His eyes came back at me focused into a point, and his anger drew his entire face tight when he said something he shouldn't have, I suppose, to his preacher—words I won't repeat about Lenny. It wasn't meant simply to shock. It was real.

"What do you know?" I asked.

"I can't tell her nothing," he said. "Nobody can."

"Alan," I said, and his eyes came back to my face. "Maybe you ought to ask."

So he did, in a way.

One Saturday night, Lenny Bolstad came out of River Road doing something near seventy, people say—but who knows? Whatever the speed, it was too fast for the curves that follow the snaking path of the Big Sioux. He considered himself an expert cyclist, but his ability to lean his own dream bike through the curves that night was checked by a frustrated anger so intense he forgot himself and even his beloved Kawasaki.

He hit a tree, and he was wearing no helmet. When the doctors put him back together, his elbows were almost gone and he had, for the most part, lost the use of his arms because his recklessness also took out something of his mind. No one knows exactly how much yet, but some of his coordination is gone, and, for now at least, so is his ability to hold up his end of a conversation. Today he sits, mostly, and watches television. If he remembers the accident at all, he's never brought it up. The doctors believe that whatever memory of that night that might still be there will likely never emerge, buried in the debris when he pinwheeled off his bike and left it ditched and twisted, like so much gnarled shiny trash. That story, it seems, his mind won't allow him to recall.

To some of the employees at Barneveld Plastics, where Lenny Bolstad worked, late-night catfish angling is the real living to which work is only a dreary prerequisite. You take a couple of poles, set them up with a forked stick in the sand at the river's bank, and weight the lines down so the nightcrawlers or grubs or whatever artificial bait you're using loll fat and scrumptious-looking on the river bottom. Then you make a fire on the bank, down a hot dog or two, roast a couple of s'mores, drink a little beer, and just spend the night. If you've got a girl along, you take a sleeping bag. Sometimes you catch fish, sometimes not.

Lenny always wanted to drive the eighteen-wheelers he and his crew loaded all day long, but he was stuck with a drunk driving charge a year ago, and the company wouldn't let him behind the wheel of one of their semis, they said, until he was old enough *and* he straightened out his act. So five days a week and half a day on Saturday, his job consisted of stacking the dozens of plastic lawn ornaments Barneveld Plastics makes. Like the other single guys on the crew, most of the day, every day, he dreamed about late-night catfishing at the river—with a woman.

Mindy and Lenny were not in love. Lenny Bolstad, twenty-one years old, wasn't looking for a wife—"just a honey," as he liked to tell his friends. Mindy is only seventeen. She has beautiful features—dark, almost piercing eyes and a perfect nose, like her brother Alan, her twin. But unlike him, she's just a bit overweight. She'd not had that many dates—that is, before Lenny Bolstad. Lenny was really the first boy to pay attention.

81

Lenny was likely dreaming of catfishing and Mindy as he stacked those lawn ornaments in empty boxcars or cavernous trailers all day. He buried himself in the fantasy of what it was going to be like that night with a woman aboard a blanket he'd laid down on the riverbank, a cold beer at his side, and nothing around but a light breeze chasing through the tree-tops, maybe some lumbering old raccoon. What he saw in his mind were the leaves almost filled in; what he could almost smell was the fresh riverbank in late spring. River Bend Park was about as far away as you could get from the loading dock, so far away that if you cross the Big Sioux right there, you're in South Dakota—a whole different state, just like that. That's what he was probably thinking.

So with everything I know about those kids, with everything I've heard and what I can imagine, this is likely what happened. Once he had a fire started, he baited the hooks and put in the lines. Then he washed his hands in river water, even brought along those little wet napkins for Mindy. He'd stuck beer in the current, tied it with an extra stringer, made her a hot dog, and spread it with ketchup and mustard squeezed from those little packets he'd collected for just this kind of night.

It was warm, even jacketless-warm, the dark sky spread out through the limbs of the trees on both sides of the river like a blanket of stars. The small fire popped and cracked, threw jumbled shadows of just the two of them over the spread of grass on the riverbank.

Slowly things rose to the point Lenny had planned all day long, nothing left to say and nothing left to happen but what the guys loading trucks always say just comes naturally. He knew it would happen, of course, and so did Mindy. He'd joked a lot, clowned around with the bait, drunk the first beer politely, then pulled her close like he'd done before as she lay her head in the crook of his arm.

Mindy Brink knew very little about love. What she under-

stood that night was that someday—not yet maybe, but someday—this guy, Lenny Bolstad, who had a better side than most
people thought, a caring side, might be someone she could love.
But at the same time she was sure, even as she lay in his arms,
that although they'd been seeing each other for almost two
months, she didn't love him—not that kind of real *love* love she
imagined she'd feel someday. That much she knew, even though
she'd never really acknowledged it, even to herself.

What she loved was the feast he'd laid before her, his prepa-
ration, his care. She loved being considered worthy of every
little thing he'd done. She loved his attention, something
she'd never received before from a guy. She loved finding
something sweet in him when everybody—including her parents—worried about them, not because of her, but him.

"You comfortable?" Lenny asked with his hand on her,
touching her as tenderly as Lenny Bolstad was capable of
touching anything in this world.

She didn't quite dare say yes, so she simply smiled wide
enough for him to see it in the darkness. From here on, she
knew, the only way for her to proceed was to feel her way
along as though that night were the dark riverbank in front
of them. She'd not made her mind up about how far this all
was going to go, not tonight at least; her not knowing put
her at a disadvantage, because all day long in those empty
boxcars, Lenny had made up his mind exactly what it was he
would be after that night.

All Mindy knew, even as she lay there beside him, was a
kind of unfocused fear that moved almost seamlessly into the
joy she felt at being loved. She understood that if he were per-
sistent, nothing she might do that night could be accomplished without a cost, and that she certainly could lose, either
way. If it ended without his getting what he wanted—and she
knew what that was—it would have been her choice, not his.
If it ended the way he wanted, whatever pleasure she might

have would come at a very dear price. The decision, she knew, was hers that night. So she was the only one with real freedom, scary freedom, Lenny already sailing along a path he'd long ago predetermined. She was four years younger than he was, but hers was the tough role, and she knew it.

So when she removed his hand, she did so not as if to admonish him, but to tell him to be careful since she was afraid. She moved it carefully, as if not to dispossess him.

Lenny Bolstad likely never understood Mindy Brink. Most of what he'd thought about women was gleaned from what he'd heard loading trucks or watching television. He assumed that if he planned the whole thing right and tried to be more loving than he would have cared to describe to his buddies on the skid loaders—with little wet napkins, ketchup in sanitary packets—if he did all of those things right, she'd love it—and him. Of course he held a very uncomplicated definition of what *love* meant, especially late at night at the river.

Her toying with him, he expected. She tried to restrain him with giggling, as if what he was up to were only a bout of tickling. But he kept after her as the fire diminished and the night slowly spread over them like a heavy wool cape. The longer they were at it, the more she understood how much at risk she was out there with a guy she didn't *love,* a man capable, by physical strength alone, of doing exactly what he wanted. Her fear rose, with good reason. She warmed to him, yet feared him, more and more.

"Mindy," he told her baldly, "I love you."

She knew it was only half-serious, although he was probably not lying to himself. She knew there was nothing she could say in response because she wasn't going to lie. So she tried to communicate something endearing with her hands, by running her fingers up and down his sides.

"I do," he said again. Then, "What's wrong?"

She turned her head.

"You don't love me?" he said.

She bit her lip and smiled.

"Well, talk," he insisted.

She didn't want to talk, so she did what she thought he might understand—she gambled that somewhere in him she could find a place to hide. She took his face in her hands and she kissed him softly—a kiss of thanks really, for not pushing her too hard.

He held her there a moment, his arms around her, then kissed her just as softly in return, confident that what she was asking him for in that warm gesture was more tenderness. He stopped kissing her and looked into her eyes, and when he did, her spirit rose with her trust, knowing he'd translated perfectly the intent of that wordless kiss. Minutes passed, Lenny holding himself at bay, Mindy breathing more easily, even thanking him for understanding, kissing him again and again for slowing, her lips softly on his.

He pulled back slightly and slid his hands along the sides of her face, tucking her hair gently behind her ears.

"Lenny," she said, the only word she dared to say, and slid her arms around him. She had never been loved by anyone, not really—not like this, she thought.

Lenny Bolstad held himself back for what seemed to him to be hours, her body close to his, his almost irreproachable fingers playing deftly against her cheeks. He restrained himself nobly, he thought, toyed with her, as she had toyed with him, cared for her, until, finally, just as he'd imagined it, with a certain kind of gentle kiss, he felt her body respond to him as if on its own, something he'd never felt before.

Lenny knew that was his cue. He'd done it all perfectly, his gentleness prompting her to offer herself the way he knew she would eventually. So he lowered himself down, just the way he'd imagined it, then put one arm behind her, around her, and pulled her down beside him.

To Mindy, to be resting on the ground brought even more relief, and she laughed, brought her hands up to his face, and kissed him hard. She held him there until she felt his hands reaching in a motion so quick she had no time to stop him. She let him have his way for a moment, almost as a means of thanking him. Then suddenly and shockingly, she felt his hands lock around her, and she knew, without even thinking, that she was in great danger. Everything changed.

She arched her back and pushed hard against him, then got to her knees and pulled her hands to her face because she couldn't look at him—wouldn't.

"What's the matter?" he said, twisting himself away.

She covered her eyes with her hands. It was so unexpected and yet so awfully predictable. She hated herself for letting go. What a fool, she thought. She'd played along too far. She couldn't speak because she didn't know what to say except the words she did right then, words that came out without her thinking: "I want to go home," she told him, turning her back. "I want to go *now.*"

Lenny Bolstad sat up quickly. "You what?" he said, angrily. "We just got here. I got lines in the water. It took me an hour to get all this set up."

She wouldn't look at him.

"You can't do that," he snarled. "I'm not taking you home. I'm sorry."

Everything had changed in a moment, in an instant, so she struggled to her feet and took the only path she could, headed for the sound of the river. He reached for her, but she pulled away and ran into the darkness.

"Mindy," he said, his voice raised. And then, "I'm sorry."

But she'd already seen his deception. She couldn't turn back, could neither speak nor face him after what he'd done, after what she'd done; so she ran toward the bend in the river, away from the fire, and climbed the bank into the grove of trees that towered from the edge, using her hands on the steep floor of the woods. The old leaves were damp, not noisy, but to her the only path was the one running away from the scene on the bank. What lay ahead was darkness, but what lay behind was worse.

"Mindy!" he yelled.

She looked back to see his outline against the fire on the bank.

"You're being stupid!" he shouted.

All she knew was that she had to get away from Lenny Bolstad, from what she had felt for him, from how wrong she'd been, how stupid she was to think that he really loved her, that he cared—all of that was there at the fire on the bank. She slid behind the trees.

By the time he came after her, he had already lost her in the darkness. What triggered Lenny's rage was only partially the frustration of her suddenly putting a stop to what he'd planned all day long. What put him back on the bike was the fact that she wouldn't say anything, even when he pleaded with her as he stood near the fire. What made him furious, really, was his frustration at her *no*—and her silence.

He reached for his flashlight, even though he knew that by carrying it lit she'd know exactly where he was in the darkness. He climbed the bank toward the cottonwoods, the sound of the river coming up in noisy whispers from the spot where a tree had been upended nearby.

"Mindy!" he yelled. "This is really stupid."

She stayed hidden. She could see him and hear him, but there was nothing he could do to find her. He searched behind upturned stumps, circled the biggest trees. Where the banks fell steeply to the river's edge, he slashed down toward the water with the beam of light. With every moment of her silence he felt more reviled, and his screaming, his swearing, grew. Circled by darkness, with nothing around him but the black outlines of trees, he kept yelling her name.

"Okay," he said, snarling, "if you're going to be that way, I'm taking off. Stay here and rot—if you're going to be so stupid." He cussed and swore, then headed back toward the smoldering fire, where the poles sat motionless on the bank. "Mindy!" he yelled once more, as if she were right beside him, "I'm not kidding. I'm leaving," he said, more quietly. Then he threw the flashlight down and walked away, left everything the way it was—lines in the water, fire going, beer cooling in the river.

He got on his bike and flexed the engine until the roar seemed almost deafening through the trees, then swung it back onto the road, the whole show a demonstration meant only for her, a scared little girl hidden away. Only then did she yell—only when she couldn't be heard.

He ran that cycle's engine up, speed-shifted through what gears he could manage, until finally Mindy heard the sudden surge and howl before the splash of metal and the silence that followed so quickly she doubted, for a moment, that everything that night had even happened.

She spoke his name again, then repeated it louder and louder, her voice slowly growing into a scream. As if she had the whole River Bend Park mapped in her mind, she ran through the trees and back to the bank toward the fire, then up the ruts they had taken to the river's edge and out the gravel entrance to the blacktop. She ran up the steep hill without tiring, until she came to a spot where a blue wispy haze rested between trees on both sides of the road. There, she found him on his back, moaning, a few yards from the tree that must have stepped up from the bank to take him, the taillight of the bike still glowing in the ditch.

The ground was wet where he was lying, and he was wet in her arms when she held him, a raspy sound in his throat with every breath. "Lenny," she said. "Lenny, listen—I'm here." She pulled his face to hers. "I love you," she said finally, a pledge.

The girl is seventeen.

"Lenny," she said again, and pulled his face to hers. She tried to calculate how far it would be to the campground at the entrance to the park, whether she should wait for a car now or start walking, how she would ever stop crying if he would die here while she wasn't around—what she should do, what she *could* do. What she understood at that very moment was that a part of her life was now over by her own hands, by what she'd done that night—or *not* done. She recognized right then, with Lenny in her arms, how easy it would have been simply to have let it happen, to have done it, like everybody else does. What's wrong with me anyway? she asked herself. They could have been there still, on the bank, the two of them doing what he'd wanted.

She sat there alone with Lenny, simply assuming he was going to die, not because she knew anything about medicine, but because she was already certain of the immensity of the burden she would carry. He would die for her sin; he had to, because of what she'd done—or not done. It was that simple.

She sat there until the swell of lights rose through the trees above her and a truck with two fishermen came up slowly on the curve Lenny hadn't made. She pulled herself from the ditch and stood in the middle of the road.

"You okay?" one of the men said.

"He's dying," she told him, pointing.

When they got to the emergency room, she seemed almost oblivious to how full of blood she was.

No one in town knew the story exactly, but all of us inferred a great deal on the night of the accident. The two of them were something of a mismatch anyway, Mindy so shy and Lenny already in trouble more than once. In the weeks that followed the accident, people from Barneveld Calvary felt terrible about Lenny, but sympathized with Mindy for what they were sure had happened, even though no one talked about it at all.

I watched, like so many others, as Mindy Brink dedicated her life to a kid she'd never loved. From the very start, when she read books and magazines to him, he responded only with his fingers and his hands. She committed her life to him, walked him up and down the halls of the hospital, fed him, spoke to him hours on end, even visited him more than his own family did, the nurses say.

For a few months her parents tolerated her slavish behavior, something they saw as an obsession. But they'd never liked Lenny Bolstad, never trusted him—a kid so much older than their daughter, a kid with a rotten reputation. Even so, for a while they didn't try to dissuade Mindy from her daily trips. By September, she'd go every afternoon, after school days notable only for the dedicated way in which she'd suddenly begun to attend to her class work. Before the accident, she was quiet and reasonably diligent, but after that night she became a model student, attentive and mature, driven by her mission.

I tried to help her—we all did, but we were powerless. Her guilt had become, in her own mind, her salvation. She told me once how it was a blessing, how it was something sent from God, how it was a good thing that happened because it helped her to see so much.

"So much what?" I said.

"I've become a better person," she said. "I've given my life for him."

How do you talk a person out of compassion?

In Barneveld people call on the preacher when the situation seems hopeless, as if only preachers deal in miracles. The more I talked with Mindy, the more I knew I was powerless. That's why I thought maybe her brother, her twin, held a key to her soul.

Next door to the Brinks, actually an entire lot of flowers away, stands the home of Lizzie Foreman, an old schoolteacher, now long retired, who today is seen only in her garden, tending her gladiolus and begonias. The Brink kids long ago gained her favor by walking respectfully through her flower bed and, when they were little, getting down on hands and knees to help her weed. Out back stands one of the last town barns in the village of Barneveld, a place where Lizzie keeps a Model A Ford in almost mint shape. It hasn't moved in forty years, people say. Years ago, with Lizzie's approval, Alan and Mindy made that Model A their secret place.

Lizzie Foreman knew Alan and Mindy were out there in her barn a few nights ago. She could tell by the flashes of light she saw inside as she stood over her sink at the back window. Lizzie Foreman has never tried to push her way into the lives of her neighbors, but she knew very well what kind of trouble Mindy had been in. When she saw those occasional meanderings of the flashlight, she stood at the sink in that old house, put her elbows down on the counter, and prayed for what might have seemed to others to be hours. Those prayers are part of this story—those silent, private prayers.

Mindy's parents had grown frustrated and finally tired of giving their daughter the patience they thought she needed in the weeks following the accident, and that night they'd tried to speak openly about what they saw as her unnecessary sacrifice in going over to the hospital day after day after day. Any parents would have spoken up—Lenny and Mindy weren't even going steady.

What was said that night needed to be said, but the effect was awful. Mindy reacted to their criticism of her love with a bitter defensiveness that created a scene in which harsh words became the only mode of communication. Grace was jettisoned in that explosion, and that's what made Alan nod to Mindy, an unspoken signal, then wander through Lizzie's flower garden with his sister to the old barn.

Alan says he put both hands up on the wheel of that old

Model A and looked around as if he were waiting for a light to change. He didn't know what to say, so he just started in with something dumb. "I wonder if she'll let me drive this thing someday," he said. "You think?"

Mindy sat back angrily. "Won't run anyway," she snapped. Coming out to the barn had been his idea. She reached up to unclasp the windshield and swung it open.

"Drive it in parades maybe," he said. "I mean, nobody'd ever use a car like this anymore. It belongs in a museum."

"What'd you want to say to me anyway?" she asked him, still seething. "I got the whole Revolutionary War to study."

"I had to get you out of the house," he replied.

"Less than a year and I'll be gone," she told him.

On that line he started in, because he was angry too. "No, you won't," he said. "You're stuck with him now."

"With Dad?"

"No," he said, "with Lenny."

The bitterness had hardly been put to rest, so she came out slashing. "I'm not *stuck* with him, Alan—geez! I love him. Doesn't anyone understand that? What do I have to do to prove that to you, anyway? Isn't it clear?"

He let those words ride up and out of the interior of that Model A and then seep out from between the cracks in the old barn because that night he had something he wanted to tell her, something he'd never brought up before. "I went down there the night it happened," he began. "I went down to where it all started—by myself. Everybody was at the hospital anyway, and I just figured something probably got left behind."

Mindy was beyond public tears, so she didn't suddenly break down. What Alan did with what he told her, however, was weaken her defenses. "You went to the river?" she said, nonplussed.

"Somebody had to. I knew all that fishing stuff was still there. I mean, somebody had to like, clean up."

She turned toward him.

"I ate your Hershey bars," he said, chuckling. "Before I found the lines, I had this stupid idea that I'd catch this monster catfish and have to throw it back because I couldn't, like *tell* people, you know? So it says in the paper, 'Alan Brink Snags Record Catfish; Lenny Bolstad in Hospital.'"

"I suppose you drank the beer," she said.

He grimaced. "You had beer?"

"He put it on a stringer in the river."

"I never saw the beer," Alan said. "I got the sleeping bag in the trunk—still there. I threw the bait away long ago, but I've got the gear. Threw the buns away right away. The way I figure, you had a hot dog and he had two—three buns out of the bag."

She turned away. "I've got to study history."

He grabbed her arm, wouldn't let go yet. "I sat there that night and looked across the river and figured out how you could have walked across over there and you'd have been in South Dakota, you know?" he said. "'That's all you got to do,' I thought, 'is walk across and you're in a whole different state.' It's all you needed to do to get away."

"A lot of good that would have done," she said.

"I don't know," he said. "I've had the feeling ever since, you know. It's like you and me, Mind, we ought to just jump start this car and take off, you know?" He slapped her arm. "You hear what I'm saying? The two of us—just leave this place. We got all kinds of reasons—"

"I got Lenny," she snapped.

"Throw some gas in this thing, bang it right out of the barn here, and take off, like Mary Poppins. Maybe go to Denver," he said.

"So what do we do in Denver?"

"I don't know—live on the street," he said, slapping the wheel. "We'll find something." He laughed.

93

She pulled her legs away, turned to look out the window. "I owe him, all right?" she said. "Why don't you just let me be?"

What her brother knew was that she'd left something behind at that river, just like Lenny had, but he didn't know what. "There was beer there?" he said. "True?"

"I wasn't drunk."

"That's not what I'm saying. You told me there was beer there—"

"In the river."

"Let's go."

"Don't be ridiculous."

"No, I mean in *our* car."

"I'm not going back there," she stated.

"How am I supposed to find it if you aren't along?"

"I'm not going."

"We've been there a hundred times. You scared of a river?"

"How can you say that?" she said. "Don't you care about me? Don't you even care that I'm full up to here with what happened?"

"Then *I'm* going," he said, putting on a macho voice. "Gonna get me some beer." He grabbed the wheel with both hands. "Staked in the river, huh? I bet I can find it. Gonna do some serious partyin'." And just like that he was out of that old car and halfway through the flowers.

It worked. She went with him.

When the lights in the barn were out, Lizzie Foreman put some tea on the stove and offered some thanks, hoping that something good had gone on inside her old useless car.

The road from Barneveld to the state line is totally unremarkable, a flat swath of concrete that floats so evenly on the gently rolling hills of cropland that it seems laid there by something airborne, slowly moving west. But the prairie bunches up like a throw rug, hills rise and fall more steeply

94

the closer you come to the Big Sioux, and the thick rows of tall corn recede, then fade, into stiff grassland. On both sides of the road that September night, corn and soybeans waved in southern breezes that carried moisture up all the way from the Gulf like a giant river unseen.

When they turned in toward the park, Mindy didn't remember leaving the place after the accident, even though she must have passed the park sign on the blacktop while in the back of the ambulance. The whole trip to the hospital was gone, even though she remembered holding Lenny in the ditch, remembered the faces of the men who stopped, even remembered the way the tall one spit before getting back in the truck.

At the top of the ridge, before the road begins to turn through the trees, two park lodges stood blackly against the bright night sky on the edge of the hill, and the moon's glaze lay over the woods beneath. A few travel trailers were parked in diagonal lines, yellow bulbs hanging in strings from canvas porches stretching over their picnic benches.

Alan drove much more slowly than he normally did. "I got here long after the bike was gone," he told her. "I think it was maybe one o'clock or something. Nobody here—dark as night."

"It *was* night, stupid," she said.

He took his eyes off the road just for a second. "I couldn't even find the spot of the accident. No lie. Took me 'til the next day. You can see it in the daylight. There's marks on the tree. Got tree tar on it now."

"What do you do—come down here all the time?" she snapped.

He hit the brakes lightly so they came to a slow stop. "All there is today is tar on the tree," he told her. "Want to look?"

"How can you do this?" she said. "Why are you trying to hurt me?"

He reached for the radio and turned it down.

95

"I'm surprised he missed the curve," Alan said. "It's not that sharp."

"He wasn't drunk—if that's what you're thinking," she told him.

He pulled away quickly because he realized that she was having some difficulty holding back tears. "That's right," he said. "I came to get the beer." He was pushing her in a way that only a brother, maybe only a twin, could do.

"I'm not getting out of the car," she said when he kept going down to the river bottom. "Don't even ask, Alan. I'm not getting out."

"The flashlight was still on," he said. "That's how I found the spot—I found the flashlight." He laughed. "Had to have Coppertops. I ought to check. I still got it."

When she didn't speak, he looked over and wondered whether he'd suddenly lost her, because her silence grew the closer they got to the bank of the river. Her eyes glazed into a stare, even though around them was nothing but darkness.

"Quiet down here," he said.

"Why are you going so slow?"

"It's a dangerous road," he replied.

"Why do you want to hurt me?" she insisted. "How come you're always saying things like that—'it's a dangerous road.' Why are you doing this?"

He turned right once they reached the bottom, kept moving along a road that led back east toward the picnic area, back to the spot he'd found that night, after the accident. "I picked that flashlight up and I looked all over the place," he told her. "Some kind of two-gun Harry I must have been, 'cause I had my own flashlight along too—one in either hand."

"What did you think you'd find?" she said.

He shut off the radio and opened the window. "I don't know," he said. "Something to prove something. Maybe underwear."

"Well, you didn't," she stated firmly.

He shook his head.

"You think you got every last thing figured out, don't you?" she exclaimed. "Everybody's got it all figured out—what happened, but no one really does. I love him, all right? Why can't people get that into their thick heads?"

"I know what happened," he said quickly.

She grabbed his arm. "He's screwed up for the rest of his whole life, and you're wondering whether or not I did it with him? That's the whole purpose, isn't it? Getting me down here?" She let him loose and turned back toward the window and said it out loud, as if there were others just beyond the rim of darkness. "I *didn't,* all right? But what's the big deal if I did anyway?"

"I don't care," he said.

"What do you mean, you don't care?"

"If you did," Alan said, "that's one thing, okay?" He pointed into her face. "But he tried to rape you—that's what happened, isn't it?" It finally came out in what must have seemed to her like an accusation. "The guy tried to rape you and you wouldn't let him," he continued, "and when you wouldn't, he got mad and got on his bike like a maniac. He tore out of the woods and missed a curve, and now it's all a mess because you got the blame, Mindy. You took it yourself, and you don't deserve a bit of it," he said. "That's the story. You don't have to kill yourself if he tried that, Mindy. That's the story here, isn't it? It was attempted rape—you can't lie.

"And now you feel awful because he's messed up and you're still in one piece and if you'd just have let him do it—right here, Mind, almost at this very spot—if you'd have just let him have his way, every last thing would be hunky-dory." He reached for her hands and squeezed them hard. "He'd still have a full deck and you wouldn't have to spend half your life reading books to him. That's it, Mind, isn't it? It's time somebody dares to say it."

97

She pulled herself away. "Will you let me wipe my face?" she said, and she opened the glove compartment to look for tissues.

He brought the car back onto the pavement, then gunned it another few hundred feet, where he parked it up near the white posts at the end of the road. He swung the door open, and the interior light spilled embarrassment all over her. "Come on," he said as he got out. "Let's go." He kept his door open to make the light unlivable. "Let's find that beer."

"I'm not going," she said. "I didn't even want to come down here, and now you want me out of this car—I'm not going."

"Okay, don't," he said. "Just go on the way you are, blaming yourself for everything that happened when it was all his fault. He's the dork that got on the bike and went screaming out of here. He's the one who tried to rape you—"

"He did not," she interrupted. "It wasn't rape."

"Don't give me that," he told her.

"It wasn't," she repeated.

"It was too."

"I was there, Alan," she said. "You don't know everything."

"It's your mind playing games. You got it all messed up." He wouldn't believe her. He tipped his head toward the river. "C'mon," he said, "we're going down there. You can't go on like this, Mind—I won't let you. You're my sister." Once again he grabbed her hand, then pulled her out of the car, and she went with him. She held herself back, but she allowed him to lead her, Alan told me. And she was crying.

The longer you stand in the darkness, the more you see, and soon enough outlines of trees against the night sky formed slowly, as if the landscape's features were appearing on a print agitated in developer. Behind them lay the flat plain of the picnic grounds, bordered to the north by a river unseen behind the deep frown of a bluff. Alan took his sister's hand and led her toward the spot where it all had happened, through the trees at the edge of the river. He held her hands up as they waded through hip-deep weeds to a spot where only grass grows beneath the limbs of a cottonwood draping the bank.

"I'm not doing this," she said, in uneven breaths full of tears.

"There is no beer anymore," he admitted, stopping. "I did find it that night. I could tell every last thing that happened from what was left around here—it was like a mystery except it wasn't one." They stood now at the bank of the river. "He dragged you down here and tried to get you drunk, Mind, and then when it didn't work, he tried to rape you." He tightened his hold around her arm. "I found the cans in the sand. I know what he was up to—I'm a guy, Mind, I *know*." He was terribly angry himself now. "You don't have to cover for him—what he did is his business, between him and God. But you don't have to do what you're doing to yourself if you did the right thing—that's what I'm trying to say." And then he let her go.

She slumped to the ground and brought her knees up high enough in front of her to hide her face and hugged her legs with her arms.

"I *know* that's what happened," he said. "Don't even try to excuse him, all right? I know guys, Mind," he told her. "I'm one of 'em."

She tightened her lips and through her tears looked up the riverbank and into the trees where they'd been that night.

"I sat here and I drank your beer myself," Alan said. "Two cans. I found the place he stuck them, and I drank them right on your sleeping bag. I saw the whole thing happen right in front of me, I swear." He let her alone and walked right up to the bank and faced the river. "Lenny? I hate him. I don't care. I know what he tried to do." He was so sure of the truth. "You don't owe him a thing, Mind," Alan insisted. "You don't. Not after what he tried to do. I can't stand the way you worship him almost—"

"I don't worship him," she cut in.

"Well, whatever it is that makes you go over there—"

"I *don't* worship him," she said again.

"Then how come you go over there all the time?"

She came off the ground and grabbed him at the shoulders. "Because it wasn't rape!" she screamed. "Because it was my fault too," she said. "Can't you get that into your head? It was my fault too. He did *not* try to rape me, Alan," she said, slowly. "You can't just blame him because I was part of it too."

"How?" he said.

So much had passed between them already that Mindy didn't hesitate. "Because just for a minute something in me told him *yes*," she said.

Alan stared into her face.

"And because I lied too—with my body."

"What do you mean?"

Her eyes were closed even though her fingers were ripping into his shoulders. Then something broke, Alan said. Her fingers reached around his shoulders and she fell against his chest. "It wasn't only his fault—what happened," she said. "Don't blame him alone because you can't."

He hadn't even imagined his own sister's complicity. But he knew through her hands on his arms that this confession had come straight from her soul, and that bringing her here had taken something from her, something Lenny had put there, even though he'd left in rage thinking nothing at all had happened.

"But you stopped it, Mindy," he told her. "You did the *right* thing."

"What's the *right* thing, Alan?" she asked. "You tell me that, will you? What on earth is the right thing? I wish I knew. My goodness, he is what he is for the rest of his life. Is that right— his life for my *no?*"

He put his arms around her. "His life for his own stupid anger, Mind," he said, "but not for your saying no. I won't let my sister hang herself for doing the right thing."

Just beside them, the river flowed by so quietly it seemed completely undisturbed by their presence.

"You'd have married him?" he asked. "Tell me, sis, were you planning on marriage?"

She never moved her head.

"Before God, would you have taken him as your husband?" he insisted.

"No," she said. "No, no, no, no."

"Then why now?"

"Because it was my fault too—"

"For saying no?"

She nodded.

He'd come to the core of everything, even though when he told me the story I'm not sure he understood it all himself. Sadly enough, to Mindy, not doing what Lenny had wanted had made them one flesh nonetheless.

Alan got to his feet and stood at the edge of the river, left his sister alone slumped on the grass behind him. Behind him, he heard her breathe heavily. The moon was shining brightly, the bank on the other side wholly visible in the wash of its light.

"He didn't have to leave," he told her. "He didn't have to fly up the road, and he didn't have to miss the turn, Mindy," he said. He turned back to his sister. "Whatever it was you did or didn't do, it wasn't all your fault."

She got to her feet and stood beside him. For a moment they just stood there, listening to the flow of the river. In the moonlight, the banks on the other side swelled like tiny bluffs, South Dakota.

"You ever go in the river?" he asked.

"What do you mean?" she said, confused.

"It's an easy question," he said. "Did you ever go in the river?"

"You mean like *go,* as in to the bathroom?"

"No—*go* as in *wade?* Don't you understand English?"

She pulled herself away. "No. I never like, walked in the river. It's mucky, isn't it?"

"You should have been a Boy Scout," he said.

"I didn't qualify."

"We used to camp down here, in Scouts." He grabbed her hand and took her to the river's edge. "You guys sold cookies—we got River Bend." He pointed out into the river. "There's this sandbar—right there, I swear it," he pointed. It's right there in the river. We used to play football out there in the mud—the guys. We used to play whole games out there—that's how big it is, this sandbar."

"Big deal," she said.

He took ahold of her hand. "I'm taking you out there 'cause you missed something not being a Boy Scout," he said, then sat down beside her and took off her shoes, then his own.

"I don't want to walk in the river," she protested. "It's full of crabs."

"Come on," he told her. "Trust me. There's this huge sandbar out there." He reached for her feet like he used to when they were kids—pulled them right from under her, and she went down in a pile.

"We're going to walk to South Dakota," he said. "C'mon—both of us."

And so they did.

A man named Harry Boorden, a retired city worker, came to the river that night and quietly took his fishing gear out of the trunk of his car. He's got one of those flip-up lawn chairs with no legs that he puts right on top of that box full of gear and food, so he's got a back to lean against when he's got his lines in the water.

Under his right arm he's got his poles, and he's sort of kicking along that big cooler toward the river, his lawn chair folded under his left arm, cap down tightly on his head, when he hears this noise—water splashing, kids yelling, so much racket he figures there's probably not a catfish from River Bend to the Klondike Bridge. So he drops all his stuff twenty yards or so from the river and hikes down to the bank in silence.

Now Harry Boorden's been at the river when a gang of kids had a keg set up somewhere in the woods. He's seen kids cavorting in the back of pickup trucks, and it's made him wonder whether all the churches they have in Barneveld really do a dime's worth of good—at least that's what he tells his friends.

He's seen kids in the river before, and at all hours. But what he saw that night was two kids hamming it up, good-natured fun, actually. He watched them long enough to be sure it was good-natured and both of them had clothes on, since you never know nowadays, and besides, he's seen that too.

He watched them for some time, getting close enough so that finally he picked out who it was down there carousing. It was the Brink kids. They were Brink kids all right. It hadn't even been that long ago that the girl had been part of the accident in which the Bolstad boy got mangled—miserable kid anyway, Boorden thought; and all of it happened right down there. It made him wonder why on earth that young lady would want to come back to this place so fast. What was it now—just a few months ago? He didn't understand how she could be playing around in the river as if it were so much fun.

He watched them walk all the way to the other side, as if they were on a hike, wading through the river and looking for holes before they took another step, all the way to South Dakota.

The next morning, Harry Boorden told his wife what he'd seen, how those Brink kids were goofing off in the river of all places, making a scene and chasing catfish all the way to the Missouri River.

"The Brink twins?" his wife said. "Are you sure?"

And that's the way the story got out—how Alan and Mindy,

quite late at night too, were splashing around as if they were crazy down at River Bend Park, of all places.

Mindy still visits Lenny Bolstad quite regularly, but not long ago she got a scholarship from a college out of state, and she accepted it. I recommended she take it myself. I recommended her for admission too, for that matter. Most everyone thinks it's a good deal for her, but nobody says as much, at least not publicly.

I don't know that anybody really understands Harry Boorden's spin on the story of a couple of strange kids one night in River Bend Park—those Brink twins, goofing around together like that at night in the water of the Big Sioux. But I like to think that that late-night trip across the river was something that just had to happen, because I remember what Lizzie Foreman told me about praying over that sink in the back of that old house that very night.

I'm no shaman, no witch doctor, no Merlin the magician. I certainly do not peddle miracles, like so many people think preachers do. But I know why we preachers sometimes have that reputation for dealing in miracles, because I've seen enough of life at Barneveld Calvary to believe in them myself.

The Wester Homeplace

The old house marked for demolition was the Wester place, the childhood home of Holly Wester Eidemiller, and I suppose that was reason enough for her uncharacteristic anger. The place was altogether unpretentious, as square and fortress-like as any old frame house—four good walls with ordinary windows, no gingerbread, no bric-a-brac, and only a square block of dull gray cement for a front porch, a chunk of concrete pitched noticeably west to east, as if years ago the mason had simply dropped it out front, prepoured, before moving on to another job.

The old front yard of Holly Eidemiller's homeplace has been owned by Barneveld State Bank for years. The board of directors bought it in 1968, a piece of ground that was home to a healthy stand of cottonwoods that people say bathed Main Street in fleecy down every June and shade all summer long.

This year the bank wanted the house. Because Holly is the kind of woman most preachers would nominate for sainthood, what made her public outrage at the bank's offer so mystifying was the fact that long ago her mother had already sold the more charming chunk of the lot—its sprawling front yard and towering cottonwoods. At that time already, the sale of the house must have seemed predestined—to Holly at least, who always seemed to have her wits about her.

The bank was not one bit pushy about cutting a deal. For all those years, the board hadn't even approached Holly about buying the place. Only when Holly's mother was taken to the Pioneer Home was Holly even gingerly approached with an offer that seemed neither untimely nor unreasonable; the word on the street was the price was very gracious.

"Why do they have to have everything?" Holly shouted at me one sunny morning after worship. "Why on earth do they have to buy up every last thing in town?" She rolled her eyes angrily. "Don't you think someone ought to stop them? I mean, look what happened a few years ago when everything was failing."

She was referring to the farm crisis, when all the bankers in the county—men who only a few years earlier pushed growth like seed salesmen—were hunted down by bankrupt farmers with zero credit and overdue promissory notes tucked away in the cubbyholes of their workbenches.

"It makes me sick to see the bank growing like that when everybody else has to cut back," she told me, waving her hand in front of my face to try to enlist the fulsome power of the church. "It makes me plain sick."

She hadn't even heard the sermon. I could tell.

Holly Wester Eidemiller is fifty years old, although she looks thirty-five. She's lean as a quick lunch, so trim I don't doubt that if those cottonwoods were still standing she could shimmy up the trunks as quickly as she did when she was ten. She's gray around the temples and her dry skin is creased and craggy as a farmer's because she's lived so much of her life outdoors, even though she's stayed at home as a mom for most of her years. As a kid, Holly Wester spent most of her summers perched up in the cottonwoods on her long front yard. People walking back home from the post office would sometimes see her up so high they'd think of calling the fire department, but then they'd hear her whistling something from the *Mickey Mouse Club* or whatever and second-guess their own fears. Master tomboy she was, people say.

"They think they can buy me out just like everybody, but I'm not going to budge. No way! I'm going to sit still right there until I die," she said, fist up, hot as a kiln, mad as you wouldn't believe, lecturing on that church lawn to whoever's hearing aid battery still had juice after my long sermon. Standing there with cups of coffee in their hands, lots of people witnessed the whole thing. But that was her plan.

"It's just wrong," she told me. "It's evil, and they won't quit. There's not a thing I can do about it because they've got the city on their side now too."

"How?" I asked.

"They'll condemn the place. The city wants them to have a parking lot. They want the house gone."

I appreciated her misery because I've always appreciated her.

"It's the principle," she said. "I've got no choice. You tell me if that's fair?"

"No," I told her. "It's your house. It's your property."

"I won't let them do it," she insisted. "I'm not going to stand for it. I'm going to fight it, and I don't care what it costs. It's just another one of them things where the rich get richer." Then she pointed her finger. "*You* understand," she said, meaning me, the spiritual leader, a man of God, the arbiter of good and evil.

The incensed Holly Wester Eidemiller I met outside church that Sunday was not the woman I'd come to respect. She had distinguished herself the very first moment I saw her, on the night the church had scheduled a welcome for us.

The church slapped together a program—ladies trio, a song by the Sunday school kids, a couple of jokes about the city boy coming to the country—to be followed by punch and coffee and pie à la mode. It was late June, the time of year when days stretch so long you wonder if darkness is on unrestricted leave, but that night was a wonder, full of welcome and love.

107

When it was over, I walked outside to an emptied parking lot. There, just beyond the stretch of concrete, was a football game—or what I thought was football. Either football or hockey—something violent at least, I thought.

Actually, it was a game called "Capture the Flag." Holly and her husband, Ben, had scheduled an activity for the church's high schoolers; they've been youth leaders for years. So this was a welcome, right? Some kid came hauling by and stuck that rag in my pocket, a gesture as well-meant as any of a hundred handshakes. The kid jerked me by the shoulder and began to run interference for me, while directing me toward some unseen goal. I knew that if I played the warthog it would take years to gain back the confidence I'd lose right then and there, so I took off like a man reckless with the assurance of his own destiny.

At first, the kids were reluctant to hit me. But once I stiff-armed one of them, a whole posse got together and beat down the interference. I was swarmed, brought to my knees, smothered. Four or five kids peeled themselves off hurriedly until only one person was left and that was Holly Eidemiller.

"That was wonderful," she said, winking.

That's how I was introduced to Holly Eidemiller.

A week after that church service where she'd made a scene, I was in my study in the basement of the church when I heard steel on steel from the floor above. I looked up at the church calendar and was reminded of the hot potato supper the kids were putting on that night, but it was three-fifteen and school was still on. It had to be Holly.

Some retired welder had put together three big folding chair carts—steel monstrosities capable of storing more than a hundred aluminum chairs—and set it on wheels so the whole works could be rolled in and out of a storage closet. Holly had it out, and all by herself she was setting up chairs.

"Funeral tonight?" I joked, after coming up behind her in silence.

"Hey," she said, calculating, "you and I can get the tables. They're downstairs."

"Aren't you doing the kids' work?" I asked.

"They do better when somebody shows them the way," she said. She put her head down and steamed away toward the stairs with me following, sheeplike. She opened the door to the storage room where long Formica tables, heavy as lead, stood up against the south wall. "They're hard on the fingers," she said, looking down at her nails. "You man enough?"

"I'm a preacher," I told her.

"That's my concern," she said.

We did it all by ourselves, but I had my own agenda. "Sit down for a minute," I said, pointing at one of the chairs in the youth room. "Before I have a heart attack, I got a bone to pick."

She looked back at me, stopped, but never sat down.

"Here's what I'm proposing," I told her, rubbing the stiffness out of my hands. "I'm thinking I can get you and Ben, and maybe somebody like Russ Ruiter from the bank, into my study down here and hammer this whole mess out once and for all. This way there doesn't have to be any lawsuits here, no brother against sister or whatever—nobody hung out to dry."

She bristled, her eyes sharpening to a point at mine.

I kept on going. "If needs be," I said, "just the three of us. You got your rights and everything, and I'm not trying to tell you it's all your fault—but what I'm suggesting is that we try to solve our own problems down here." I pointed down at the floor we were standing on.

"This isn't a court," she said.

"I know it's not a court. That's the point—to avoid it."

"Why?"

109

"Courts get ugly," I said. "And they cost money—even if you win."

"I'm not scared," she said.

"I'm not saying you are," I told her. "I'm suggesting there may be a better way here, a less public—"

"I'm not shy either," she interrupted. "I haven't done a thing wrong but put my mother in the Home. If you think I'm worried about what people think—"

"I'm not."

"Then I've got nothing to fear. It's the American way, isn't it?" she said. "Law and justice and all of that."

"What's the point?"

"The point is nobody ought to get thrown off their property just because the bank wants to make a parking lot. That's the point, padre," she explained. "Let me get the bank in court—I'll win that one." She stood away from the chair. "Shoot," she said, "what jury's going to find for the bank when they're taking on this fifty-year-old woman and her elderly mother." She pointed her thumb toward her chest. "The bank doesn't have a prayer."

"I'm trying to be a peacemaker," I said.

"There's a time for peace," she told me, "and a time for war." Then she walked right out of the room.

Right about then, kids started coming in the front door, half of them plugged into Walkmans, carrying portable ovens, dishes and jugs, bags full of groceries, and pecks of potatoes. I watched Holly as she began to storm through the instructions, barking out signals and commands, the Patton of the fellowship hall—freezer paper over the tables, sauces mixed and readied to heat, potatoes washed, serving lines straightened and streamlined.

"What exactly are you after?" I asked her twenty minutes later, when she stopped to take a breath. "You want to move back into that house?"

"What do you mean?"

"You're not after more money?" I inquired.

She grabbed my arm. "I don't give two hoots for the money," she said. "And I don't care what people think—the point is, they're not getting my house." And then she said a swear word, the only one I ever heard her use, kids all around her, enough volume to be heard and then some. "I don't care. I can win this one," she said.

"That's it—winning?" I asked her.

"This time, yes," she said.

Squeals and laughter pulled her away toward the kitchen, where a squadron of fifteen-year-old kids washed potatoes, their sleeves rolled, over the open sinks.

I went to the Home to visit Holly's mother but found a Do Not Disturb sign hung from her door. When I asked a nurse about it, she said to maybe first call the desk before I came again. "Dora doesn't much care for visitors," she informed me.

The idea of people in my own church heading into a lawsuit bothered me, and I must admit some sympathy for Holly. After all, the bank—an institution Christ would likely have vilified—exerted enough pressure that Holly Eidemiller was provoked into public profanity.

I couldn't see Holly's mother that day, but while I was at the Home I spotted Jenny Mulder, who's been there for years and remains in better shape mentally than most of the others. For years already she's been in a wheelchair, but she'd hardly call herself *confined*.

"So what's new at the Pioneer Home?" I asked her. She was sitting in the sunroom on the east end with a circle of women who didn't seem tuned in to the program on the television in front of them. A wide piece of pressed wood was laid over the handles of her wheelchair, a game of solitaire spread out in front. "I hear Dora Wester's not very social?" I inquired. "I came to see her especially."

111

"The woman's got reasons," Jenny said. She brought a couple little numbers up to the row of aces on top. "You can't know any more about what goes on inside somebody like that than you can know what's in these cards." She pointed, then cracked the edges of the deck on the tabletop. "I don't think she ever got over her little boy."

I had no idea what she was talking about.

"It would have been awful enough to lose a boy in the way he went to glory, but to have that death come so quick after her husband's—nobody should have to go through that. And then the boy had such a public death."

All I'd known about Holly Eidemiller was her energy—and, recently, her anger.

Jenny put the cards down, set her elbows on the lap board, positioned her hands as if she were to pray. "When it happens in front of a crowd of kids, nobody forgets. People die here all the time, but usually there's only a nurse around." She shook her head. "But when kids see one of their own get killed the way her boy did—it's in there forever." She brought an old hand up to her temple, as if it could reposition a thought.

"What happened?" I asked gently. "I'm sorry—"

"Train. Flyer—one of them that don't stop when it comes charging through town. Gone now. Passenger trains." She scratched her chin with the top of the deck. "For years after, I never heard the nine-fifteen without thinking about the tracks being clear. It come right through the town, fifty miles an hour maybe."

"A train wreck?" I said.

"Didn't wreck the train one bit. Engineer stopped because he saw it happen, saw the boy right in front of his nose and hit the brakes—you ever heard flyers come to a stop? That was before we had a local ambulance here, but anybody anywhere near town knew it had to be something bad, such a screech that thing put up."

112

"Dora Wester had a boy who got hit by a train? Holly's brother?"

Jenny nodded. "And she lost her husband not more than four or five years before. Heart attack. Wasn't even fifty. A welder downtown at Les Maarten's. Fell over at work. Today they'd find a reason and somebody would sue, but back then they said his heart just stopped working. I think we're better off not knowing sometimes."

"Her husband?" I asked, still taking this in.

"Jake."

"And then her son?"

"Killed in town on the night the kids were making homecoming floats. For the parade—homecoming parade. For the football game the next night. It was Thursday, the day before homecoming for everybody except little Herbie Wester, who had his homecoming the night before, you might say." She fixed her eyes on me. "My word, I'm talking like an old woman, ain't it so? Getting all mixed up and you not knowing a thing. But it's hard to imagine anybody wouldn't know."

"He got hit by a train?" I asked again.

"That ain't the worst of it." She looked around as if someone might be listening. "It was a game they were playing. My Kenny told me later, my son. Boys played 'Chicken' is what they called it—who can cross the tracks last, who dares."

She let that sit for a minute, stared me down.

"It wasn't an accident?"

"You don't call that an accident? He's a boy, Reverend," she said to me. "He's just a boy. I call that an accident."

"One of them jumps and then another? You mean, it was Russian roulette or something?"

"Russian what?"

"I mean, almost like suicide."

"Call it an *accident*. If you don't, it hurts way too much, even now, even after all these years."

"And his mother? She didn't take it well—his mother?"

"Would you?"

"I didn't mean it that way," I told her.

"She wasn't a strong woman to start with."

"How old was Holly?"

"Girl."

"Younger?"

"Younger, but stronger. Always was." The old woman shook her head. "You know how hard that woman can work? You ever seen her work?"

"Sure," I said.

"That woman can work like a man."

There was a time in my life when I considered a future in the ministry to be something almost idyllic. I pictured myself working through the New Testament all week long with maybe a half-dozen top-notch commentaries and some state-of-the-art concordance on a CD-ROM. I never worried about how a preacher in a town as small as Barneveld might spend his week, because if I loved anything at all it was mixing it up with God's Word. What I never thought I'd be is a detective, but sometimes that's the work I do.

Armed with what Jenny had told me, I nudged the Herbie Wester story into conversation whenever I could in the next week or two, trying to throw some light on a death that was almost forty years behind all of us, except the Westers. And everybody knew something, even those who weren't alive in 1957.

Alvinah Westerbeke, seventy-three, remembers the entire freshman class walking in a single line from the old high school to the church, two blocks away, in almost perfect silence. She'd watched them from the jewelry shop, and she remembers how odd it was to see all those high school kids walking so peacefully you'd have thought they were dazed—because they were, she says.

Bert Nonhof was only ten years old, too young to have been anywhere near the train tracks that night. He claims that the story of Herbie Wester's death made such an impression on him that even today he can see it happen, just as if he were there. He still sees it.

Clarence Walraven, fifty-six, remembers being one of the kids making a float that night. He remembers how the teachers who were supervising knew right away something horrible had happened when the train screamed. By the time he got there somebody had covered the body with a blanket. It was dark—you couldn't see much. The next day he says you felt this urge to go to see the exact spot, and yet at the same time, nobody dared. "In my mind, there's still blood on the stones right there along the track," he says.

Beth Koppers was just a child when it happened. She remembers telling her own parents how upset she was when the homecoming parade was called off, and she says she'll never forget the sermon she got, right then and there.

Freya Logterman says her mother spent hours over at the Wester home for weeks after the accident. "Of course, I had lost a sister about ten years earlier," she told me. Then she corrected herself. "I should say, 'my mother lost a daughter.' I was so young I didn't really understand." They lived just across the street.

Fern Klein, forty-eight, says for years as a child she wondered whether or not Herbie Wester went to hell for playing such a horrible game. She says she remembers lying in bed and imagining that boy in robes of fire.

Jeremy Brill says every homecoming he still thinks of it, even though he wasn't even born at the time of Herbie's death.

Avery Lasserdahl says he moved to Barneveld two years after it happened. He was in high school, and he remembers the kid's picture in a hallway display—thin and bookish—and he remembers thinking how strange it was that Holly could come from that house. "Because she was Holly," he said, "even back then."

Mike Blekkink, fifty, was in Holly's class. He remembers Holly being named homecoming queen when she was a senior, partly because nobody had forgotten what happened, and partly because Holly was—well, Holly. "It felt so good, you know, when she got queen," he says.

Ann Moray, fifty-six, says she remembers being almost obsessed about how the boys who were with him that night would feel. "It takes more than one kid to play 'Chicken,'" she said. She remembers sitting beside one of them at the funeral, seeing how broken up he was. "Even more than the rest of us," she said.

"Who?" I asked. "Can you tell me?"

"Oh, I don't remember all of them anymore, but the one that sticks out in my mind is Russ Ruiter."

Russ Ruiter, the vice president of the Barneveld State Bank.

So I found out what I could about Russ Ruiter, the bank's vice president. I discovered he's a man with a past that most members of Barneveld Calvary wouldn't be proud of. But then, neither is Russ.

He is a vice president for the simple reason that he married—his second marriage—the owner's daughter, a woman who had also previously loved and lost. They found each other in a fashion that led both of them to believe they were destined for a mutual future no matter how different they were, Russ being six years Natalie's senior, his roots, like hers, in Barneveld, but in a whole different social class. The two of them had never met in town. After moving to Chicago and suffering through a pair of bad marriages, they nursed their individual pain in the place that eventually drew them together—the church, specifically a church in Chicago they both picked because it had links denominationally to Barneveld Calvary.

At one time, Russ drank almost viciously; I knew that before. I've talked to the man, and I respect him for what he's put behind him. He knows it was his own foolish behavior that led to his first wife's picking up their children and leaving him for an unmarried lawyer she'd met in the laundry room of their apartment. By his own account, he stayed in a stupor for almost a year, even though he held on to a job as an ad exec at a third-rate radio station, where he says most of the personnel were quite frequently as drunk as he was. He was a grand salesman and made out famously in an industry where a fast mouth was the ticket to success and most of the contacts were made over booze. That's what he says.

He met Natalie in a class of losers, he says—a whole Sunday school of them, in fact—a Bible study for singles at that Chicago church. He went to church when he realized he could fall no farther without flirting with hell itself. He claims he didn't recognize her because he'd left Barneveld by the time Natalie had come through high school. But she knew him because among his other talents was a natural athleticism that made him good at just about every sport he tried, including arrogance.

It wasn't long, he says, before they found themselves, each other, and something of the values they'd both abandoned. Together they came back to Barneveld. Natalie's father didn't kill any calf or throw a great party, but once he saw his new son-in-law showing some entrepreneurial spirit, he found a way to get him into the bank, where Russ has been ever since.

Russ is slick, even today—almost too slick. When you see him, when you talk to him, you get the sense that he's seen more of real life than most people in Barneveld ever do, and in Barneveld, that characteristic alone can be scary to some people at church. Nonetheless, Natalie's father likes Russ's charisma.

Russ Ruiter is a man so slim, so proportioned, that the suspenders over his crisp white shirt make him look like something off a magazine ad, and in Barneveld that's unusual for a fifty-year-old man. His secretary opened his door when I visited him. She introduced me, then deftly began to straighten out the papers on his desk.

"She's working on my image," Russ said, pointing at her. "That's all they teach kids nowadays—image." He played with her, didn't flirt, just played lovingly. "Gretchen has a degree in business management," he told me—for her benefit, "but she's still the one making coffee."

The young woman was wearing a suit coat and slacks color-coordinated with the women out front.

"I told her to marry somebody with bucks like I did," he said, "but that's already been decided. This is Gretchen Hamlin—married to Willie, you know, of Paul." He pointed at the two of us, and Gretchen nodded politely. "It's a crime, isn't it? All that money for a degree, and she ends up working for a guy who flunked out of community college."

She snapped her head up. "I keep telling him that someday I'm going to take that chair myself."

"If I die of a stroke or something, Reverend, check the coffee," Russ said, pointing to the steam rising from his cup.

Then she was gone.

I rushed through some formalities, but Russ is the kind of man who really doesn't require softening.

"I talked to Holly Eidemiller about the bank and herself getting together some time in my office and trying to talk this thing through—about the house."

"Please do it," he said.

"I tried," I told him.

"No go?"

"Wouldn't budge. Not in the least."

"That determined, eh?"

"Wouldn't hear of it."

He shook his head. "If that house were a mansion, it'd be one thing—but it isn't," he said, almost painfully, pointing over his shoulder.

"It's a good offer?"

"Reverend, this banking business is something I'm still a little uncomfortable with." He leaned back and put his hands up behind him. "Remember, this is a guy who spent more time than I want to remember living on beer and pretzels—and I bought those on credit. Gretchen's in here straightening out papers that got numbers on 'em I don't have enough education to read. But I got a heart, all right? I wouldn't sell her short—never." He riffled through some papers.

Maybe it's his past, but there's something about him that's much less uptight than a lot of people in my congregation. "Listen," I said, "this is maybe a long shot, but I been hearing this old story lately about Holly's brother—"

"About Herbie?" He dropped his hands down to the arms of his chair as if the question itself had let out some steam. "Shoot," he said, shaking his head, "right from the start I didn't want to do this—I really didn't. Every day of my life I come to work at a building right next door to that haunted house, but I never wanted to buy it—*because* of all that." He looked down at the palms of his hands. "You know that stuff about life lines in your hands," he said, "about how long they are or something?" He looked up at me, pointing at his hand. "I got something on here that some witch would note right away," he said. "Herbie Wester's here," he said, "and there ain't a thing I can do about it."

"The kid got killed playing 'Chicken'?" I simply started the story and waited for Russ to pick it up.

For just a moment, I think he looked up at me as the outsider I always was in Barneveld. But it didn't stop him. "I like to think there's nobody around who remembers who it was exactly that was with him that night—that's what I like to think," he said.

He picked up a pencil between his fingers and dropped it like a drumstick on the desk pad. "Maybe it was my fault." He looked down, poked at his glasses with the back of his hand. "Shoot, Reverend, I was fully grown at the end of sixth grade." He pointed to himself. "Maybe I did it, I don't know."

"Nobody blames you," I told him.

"Who you been talking to?" Ruiter asked.

I shook my head. "They ought to have a book of things you have to know before you come into a town like this one— local history. I didn't know a thing, but nobody I talked to blames you."

He didn't look relieved. "It's probably just me."

"What do you know that everybody else doesn't?" I said.

"I was there, for starters," he said, nodding hard. "I can't say I saw it happen, but I was there. Nobody else."

"What do you mean?"

Ruiter pulled himself closer up to the desk. "Nobody else that was there lives here anymore, and maybe that's why."

"Because of the accident?"

"I don't know," he said. "But we used to do it all the time, and it sounds so much worse than what it was—"

"This 'Chicken' game?"

"It sounds awful. Shoot, my daughter came home from school a few months ago with the story, told us all about Herbie Wester. She picked it up in a health class, drivers' ed maybe—and it was a big deal because whoever told her said it happened right here at a certain place along the tracks in this very town. I mean it happened right here. 'What an awful story,' Angie says, and Nat is sitting on the couch reading the paper and she doesn't even look up because she *doesn't know*— she was that much younger than I was."

Still holding the pencil, Russ leaned back and crossed his arms over his chest. "And already I got this whole thing with Holly going on because the board of directors thinks we got to have that lot for parking, and the house isn't really worth that much anyway. I keep telling them they got to pay more, and they keep saying that fifteen years ago or whatever, Holly sold this whole chunk we're standing on right now, and they can't begin to understand why on earth she'd balk, especially at the sweet offer we're making. And all the time, the only way I can figure out all of Holly's fireworks is that it's Herbie behind this—his ghost, Reverend. She's blaming me for it, and maybe she's got a right to."

Guilt was thick as fog in that office, but I still didn't see the whole story—a kid on the tracks, a train, a game of "Chicken." "She *does* have a right to blame you?" I asked.

"It was my idea to grab a smoke away from all the teachers—big deal, you know? You're hanging around the floats making fun of the good-looking girls and whatnot, and then you just got to be a man, you know—got to show something. So I suggested to some guys to go out along the tracks and light up. I think I did—I don't know. I can't remember exactly what happened that night, other than that I was there when he went down. I never heard a thing, but I remember looking back and seeing him fall away from the wheels, dead. I remember that." He threw the pencil on the desk, put his elbows down, and rubbed his fingers across his eyes.

"It's a personal thing with Holly?" I asked.

"I don't know how else to figure."

"That's the whole thing?"

"What do you mean?" he said.

"I mean, what happened that night."

"That's forty years ago," he said. He rubbed his temples, ran his hands around the back of his head, and leaned back in the chair. "What I see is little more than a movie shot, I think—something my mind creates. You tell me," he pointed to his head, "what happens to a memory soaked in blood? How do you get it clean?" He shrugged his shoulders.

121

"Who else knows?" I asked.

"Me—and her, I guess. And now you."

The look on his face was a kind of grief, I think.

"I never even told Nat what really happened. I mean, what for? I was a kid," he said, purely defensive. He looked down at the pictures of his kids beneath the glass on his desk. "She never brought it up—Holly didn't. We asked her to come in—*Andy* asked her to come in because, I told him, 'I don't want any part of this, really.'"

"Even then?"

"It was already in my mind—that she was blaming me." He shook his head. "But the whole hardball stuff—getting the town council to play the game with us and everything? I don't like it." He pulled his foot up to the desk top and plunked it down. "I don't like any of it."

I needed to understand more. "What was he like—Herbie?" I said.

Russ looked around. "Truth?"

"Truth."

"Wimpy. Why do you think we called him 'Herbie'?"

"So it's all of you in a bunch," I said, trying to put it together, "and the train is coming and this big clump of kids—"

And then Russ took over. "And I jumped, and I laughed—I don't even remember if I was scared. Probably not. I was laughing, though, and then I looked and he was in the wheels—just for a minute he was in the wheel, flopping. And then he was dead."

He pushed his chair back from the desk and stood, hooked his fingers into his belt and tugged his pants up just a bit. "How can I explain it? He lost the game." He turned away toward the window facing Main. "I know it's wrong—it's an awful game. I understand that."

"Often?" I said. "You played this kind of game often?"

"With cars too. Everybody knew it. Guys did it with cars—"

"Come on—"

"I'm not kidding. It happened. And we did it too, just like we did that night, except nobody ever, ever got hurt. Only that time." He shook his head. A car came up through the bank's drive-thru, and Ruiter came back to his chair.

"You really need that property?" I said.

Ruiter laughed. "When I married Nat, I really landed with my butt in the butter. And what I learned is that you don't sit on money. It's got to get used."

Something had to be done. "You think I ought to try to get the two of you together?" I suggested. "Maybe just the three of us. What we need is some peace—I mean, for both of you."

"Wouldn't have been for a parking lot, I'd have been okay," he said. "The same is probably true of her."

"How can you say that?" I said.

He smiled, knowingly. "Don't you have something back there, Reverend?" he said. "Isn't there something you carry around with you?"

"I don't understand."

"There's things you carry until you've had them so long you don't know what it might be like without them," he said, "and they start to carry you eventually." He broke into a laugh. "You don't have to think about them to know they're there."

"What about forgiveness?"

"Really," he said. "How's that woman ever, ever going to forgive me for killing her brother? We're talking about a real flesh-and-blood human being with forty years of blame in her soul. You and me and Holly get together, you think you can straighten that out?"

"God can," I told him.

"It's not God's house we're toying with here, it's Holly's—and you've heard her."

"You're not angry with her?" I asked.

123

"What Holly did that night and for the rest of her life is heroic. I'm serious."

"What do you mean?" I said.

"Her ma never got over Herbie's death," he said. "There's a fancy name for it—maybe Gretchen knows it." He pointed at the preacher. "*You* ought to with all your education. My mother used to call it just 'housebound.' Mrs. Wester never got out. She wouldn't. But nobody blamed her—even before her old man died."

"That was just a few years before—"

"Not long. I remember that one because I was happy to see the guy go. He whipped me once. We lived in town then, and I must have got sick of Herbie—I don't remember—teased him, maybe beat him up a little. But what I remember is the way his old man followed me and slapped me up good—oh, I don't mean he hurt me, really. I remember thinking Herbie was going to get it worse from me next time for signing his old man up to fight his battles."

"Was she there? The time their dad whipped you? Was Holly there?"

"I didn't see her." He shook his head. "All I remember is that I was scared my old man would see him beating on me. My old man was no saint, Reverend, and I thought he'd take George Wester apart right there in the shadow of the steeple of the old downtown church. That's what scared me."

"Your father?" I said.

"That my old man's gone, Reverend," Russ said, "makes your job a lot easier—let me tell you that. Maybe I got too much of him in me."

"What happened that night?"

"Herbie didn't make it."

"That's the whole story?"

"He was trying to be something he couldn't be, something I pushed him to be, I suppose. But when he made that last jump, he couldn't pull it off." He kept shaking his head. "I think of it often as my fault—I really do. I teased him mercilessly."

"Maybe you ought to tell her," I said.

"What good would it do?" he asked.

"She'd know the truth," I said.

"I don't know that she's interested in that," he said. "And if I were Holly, after all this time, I don't know myself that I'd believe me—or want to. By this time, maybe there's no difference."

I walked out of the bank still carrying a fervent sense that if ever God's forgiveness was worth everything I'd considered it to be, it was capable of bringing healing to something as old and as final as the death of Herbie Wester. I wonder now if maybe I wasn't testing the Lord and his promises, insisting that everything I believed would be proven true by some cessation of Holly's bitter anger.

I found her where I thought I would, working at Marv's Lunch, one of the few businesses left on Barneveld's Main Street, a place she waitresses not because she needs the money, but because she gets to see a lot of people. I'd been warned twice about pursuing the matter—first, by an experienced preacher who told me digging up old secrets was like trying to root out milkweed, since the lateral roots of old transgressions just about make the weed impossible to kill. And now Ruiter himself said he thought clearing anything up was absolutely impossible. But I've always been impressed by the character of a holy fool, someone who keeps on going in the name of Christ, even though the walls are too high or the burdens too heavy.

When Holly brought me some water, she winked. An older woman I didn't know was waiting to pay for her food with a checkbook she had withdrawn slowly from her purse. She opened it, then turned it around and laid it on the countertop so Holly could fill in the amount. Then she tucked the checkbook back in her purse. Her cane, not a white one, went poking out in front of her as she braced for the steps at the front door.

"Poor woman thinks she can still see," Holly said when she came back to me. "What is it with people that makes them deny what they're losing? Most of the old geezers who come in here can't hear anything beneath a shout, but none of them wear hearing aids. What a world," she said. "So you can't do without coffee this morning, Reverend?" She swung the pot at me and right-sided the heavy green cup in front of me. "So what brings you out?" she asked.

"It's Herbie, isn't it?" I said. Why wait?

She put the coffee back down. "You want something with that?" she said, pointing at the coffee cup.

"Roll—cinnamon roll."

She lifted the glass panel from the pastry shelves, grabbed a paper plate from beneath the counter, then picked up a roll with long aluminum tongs.

"I think I understand," I said.

She poured what was left in the nearly emptied pot into the sink, rinsed it out quickly, and placed it beneath the coffee-maker before pouring in another pot full of water. The place was empty, really. It was almost eleven, and three older women were sitting across the room in a booth.

"I just came from Russ Ruiter," I said.

Her face was so full of hate when she turned that I wondered if confrontation had been the right maneuver. "Like nobody else maybe," I said, "you know how rotten tough it is to forgive."

For a moment she stared, judging whether or not she could trust me. "Nobody knows but the two of us," she told me.

"You and me?" I asked.

"Me and him," she said.

"Three of us—and more," I told her.

"Thirty-nine years, and every day I got to live with a lie." She turned away and crossed her arms over her chest, then started talking in a snippy voice. "Don't play 'Chicken.' Just look at what happened to that kid who died up there by the welding shop. You guys know the story? It happened right here in Barneveld, right in the middle of town." She shook her head angrily. "Every year somebody tells the story about the brainless boy who got run over by the train on a dare." She looked right at me. "Every year my brother is a moral lesson—a stupid moral lesson. Even my kids came home with it—'Don't be stupid like Herbie'—when the fact is, he was murdered."

"Murdered?" I asked, surprised at her choice of words.

"You heard me."

I knew I couldn't push her—not Holly, and not this, as old as the evil was inside her. *Murder,* I thought. *Murder.*

"What did you tell them—your kids?" I inquired.

"I lied," she said, her brown eyes tightening into something wholly colorless. "I told them their uncle was a good kid who one night got himself in a bad place, and they shouldn't think of him as some brainless hood, because he wasn't. He wasn't that at all," she insisted. "He got himself in with a bad bunch." She kept the towel in her hand as she brought her fists down quietly on the countertop. "And they said, 'Who?' Every one of my kids said, '*Who* is this bad bunch?'"

"What'd you say?"

She raised her chin. "I told them they were all gone—*all* of the guys he was with—that's what I said, and for a long time it was true."

"Then it wasn't a lie?"

"As good as," she said. "Half-truth. What I never told them was that Russ Ruiter pushed my brother with his own bloody hands." Years of anger tightened her resolve. "That's what I never said. I could have poisoned his name, but I didn't."

127

She leaned over and came in close. "Just him and me know— that's it."

"Russ *pushed* him?" I asked.

"Shoved him because he hated him. I know he hated him. Shoved him. Killed him. Threw him down in the path of that train. That's what I know."

"How?"

"I don't have to say," she said, pulling herself back up to her feet. "But I know what happened and so does he."

She grabbed the full pot off the urn and headed across the diner to the ladies, where she suddenly became Holly Eidemiller, refilling cups of coffee and flowing with the banter that earns practiced waitresses good money in cafés other than Marv's Lunch. "How's the coffee anyway?" she asked them. "Town water's been so off-color lately you'd think it came out of somebody's fish tank."

The ladies said the coffee was fine. They explained how when it was coffee you couldn't tell how yellow the water was anyway, and then they all laughed. "Besides," one of them said, "it's always better when somebody else makes it."

"And cleans up after you," Holly said, swinging the rag.

That's how she'd done it for all those years—carried the story in some iron part of her heart, smiled through life itself and covered the hurt, unmasking it occasionally, but only when she was all alone. That's how she'd nursed her sense of the truth for all those years. It had become as much a part of her as her short-cropped hair. Maybe what she'd carried actually produced her abundant energy, the intensity of that secret so explosive it had created its own kind of life.

She came back around the counter and stopped in front of me, back in a character as full of hate as anything I'd ever seen on stage, eyes fierce, full of heat and anger. She pointed at my cinnamon roll with those steel tongs. "You want me just to put that thing back? You haven't touched it."

When I nodded, she put down the pot, grabbed the cinnamon roll with the tongs, shoved it back to the place where it had been before, then smiled. "You tell me this, Reverend. How can a man who's sitting where he is even smile today?" she said. "How can he live with himself? He may think he's home free, but as long as I live, I'll always know the truth. He pushed my brother."

She stared at me with such ferocity that I knew the only force that could possibly alter her sense of what had happened was something divine, capable of turning her inside out. For forty years she'd told herself that her brother's death was murder and had thereby absolved him, and herself, of the misery. It seemed to me then that it wasn't the truth that had set her free at all, it was her version of a story that a whole town couldn't forget. And I began to think that some things, like my friend had said, were better left unexamined. What had happened in Barneveld one homecoming week was buried so deeply that maybe the best one could do is keep down the growth of hate by mowing it down, time after time after time.

Fern Klein saw me walk out of Marv's Lunch just a few minutes later, and then called the church to ask whether I was okay, because my face, she said, was as long as a hard afternoon.

My only thought was to go back to Russ, not because I was sure that I could do something about all of this, but because I assumed he ought to know that at least we were right about something—at the bottom of Holly's anger lay the death of her brother.

The holy fool in me died at that moment, got pinned by the stronger self, the voice of reason. I got to thinking there was nothing I could do.

Across the street from the bank stood a home that was quite likely built just following the Second World War. The lot was not large, but it was wooded and beautifully groomed. That house was rectangular, with two wide, latticework bay windows across the front, giving the place a slightly pretentious, New England look in a prairie town like Barneveld. A few might have called it showy, a house that looked too smart, as people used to say. Three identically sized dormers protruded from its steep roof, and on the far end—the east end—a sandstone fireplace chimney spread across what seemed half of the wall.

Most everyone in town was shocked one morning, maybe three weeks later, when a van pulled up in front of that house and a crew of three started to work. In little more than a day they moved out most of the furnishings and the widow who'd lived there; then another crew, maybe five guys, rolled up in a flatbed truck. It took them a couple of long working days to manage it, but soon enough they had that home cut—literally cut—from its own foundations and jacked up a foot or two to get huge studs beneath the frame. Then they hoisted it on the flatbed and lugged it to a new foundation on a vacant lot on the east edge of town.

The house belonged to Natalie Hermanson Ruiter's grandmother. Some of the older people in town still call the place "the banker's house" because Natalie's grandfather, like her father and now her husband, was a Barneveld banker—at that time *the* Barneveld banker. But that house was hoisted up and hauled away by a crew of house-movers from a town just over the South Dakota border. Then a few of the trees were shaved from the lot, the whole place excavated, and concrete laid down tastefully between the trees that remained.

I have no idea what Russ Ruiter might have said to convince the board of directors to drop the suit for the Wester homeplace, but the old radio salesman must have created a convincing case because in the end the bank's new parking lot ended up across the street instead of on the adjacent lot. No one would have guessed such a thing would happen. When you compare those two houses and the two lots, what the board of directors ended up doing about whatever parking problem they thought they had seemed not only unexpected but just plain stupid.

In fact, even today some still can't understand how a person as wonderful as Holly Wester Eidemiller could be so stubborn about a house that had nothing going for it other than the memories of a childhood that quite likely held very great pain.

Two years passed—not even two really, but two homecomings at least, neither of which passed without reminding me of the horrible death of Herbie Wester.

This afternoon I sat at the bedside of a woman whose children are bitter because they may very well lose a mother who'd seemed the very picture of health. Alvinah Westerbeke was critically injured in an accident, and the doctors don't hold much hope for her life. She'd parked her car in that new parking lot across the street from the bank, looked both ways before crossing, then started out slowly, carefully, as she always does.

Meanwhile, some kid angled out into the left lane on Main Street to avoid someone who was parallel parking in front of the bank. For some reason nobody knows, this kid suddenly decided to chase down Linden, taking a sharp right from what was almost the left lane on Main. He never laid eyes on Mrs. Westerbeke, not until he heard a sound he'll never forget and saw the old woman roll up and over his hood before falling to the side of the car.

Mrs. Westerbeke is in very bad shape, and the kid's a broken mess. He's now begun a life that will be haunted, like those of Holly Eidemiller and Russ Ruiter. Mrs. Westerbeke will likely die in the next couple of days; when she does, the boy's guilt will only grow.

Her daughter spoke to me about her mother's condition outside her room after I visited, and then she said this: "I'm

131

ready to sue. I really am. Everybody knows putting that parking lot across the street was dangerous. Everybody knows that. It was just a matter of time before somebody like Mother got hit. People have talked about it for a long time. Everybody knows it. I can't understand why they didn't just buy the Wester place. No one can. It's so dangerous."

Who gets the blame here? Holly Eidemiller, the saint, for investing in a version of the story she created in order to cover her horrendous grief? Or Russ Ruiter, the prodigal son, who offered mercy to atone for his sin the night of Herbie's death—whatever that sin was? Or should it be me, the preacher, who threw in the towel on his own ideals and told himself that this time the truth of something buried beneath forty years of pain was simply not worth pursuing?

Who gets sued here? Who is guilty?

We all stand in need of grace.

Adrianna Meekhof, Stuart Mackey, and Mutual Sin

For most of his life, Les Meekhof dominated people by sheer physicality and the raw power of his deeply pronounced facial features—a proud nose, piercing blue eyes, and a forehead shaped prominently like the back of a garden spade. His thick, graying eyebrows were virtually indistinguishable, even though he was almost hairless, his scalp a shiny dome. He was overweight, big-boned, and as heavy chested as any subject from the canvas of Thomas Hart Benton—and he was not well liked.

But his suicide would have been a surprise in Barneveld, had anyone known of it, because Les was thought to be a man of vision, like his father, the famed Barneveld preacher, even though Les's visions rather spectacularly lacked his father's spiritual dimensions and often as not ended up in failure.

Les was a bit past fifty when he took the longest trip of his life in a Dodge Ram pickup he'd parked for no more than an hour in his newly built service shop. If people had known he'd killed himself, they would have attributed his despair to his most recent and spectacular business failure. He'd stuck everything into the insulation business when it seemed oil prices were finally rising to the level of the world market.

They didn't, and Les, along with his payroll of forty-some men, took a dive. In a matter of months, his fleet of a dozen trucks spent more time inside the biggest steel building Barneveld had ever seen than they did delivering foam insulation to inefficient old houses as far south as Nebraska.

But it wasn't the failure of his business that prompted him to start the engine of his Dodge Ram that night. He'd seen failure before—lots of it. What began the process that led to Les Meekhof's suicide was his discovery that his wife, Adrianna—sweet, demure, loving as a mother, caring as a spouse—had carried on a short love affair with the man who'd given her a part-time job at the Foodland store downtown. It was adultery, but not his; and in legal terms not even hers.

In Barneveld, people still take the state of a loved one's soul very seriously, and nothing upsets sensibilities more than suicide because everyone knows it requires a despair so deep there can be no hope, and therefore, no faith. No one knows that better than Adrianna, whose mother hanged herself years ago in the attic space of their house. Although she never saw her mother suspended there, that image is so fixed in her mind that she says she has, after almost forty years, come to believe that she peeked through the trap door herself and saw the misshapen body.

This second suicide, her husband's taking his last breath of monoxide air, is another that Adrianna will never forget because she knows that whatever godlessness grew in her husband's soul in his last hours was planted there, at least in part, by her own hands.

And what had she done?

To call what happened between Stuart Mackey and Adrianna Meekhof an *affair* is to mislead. What happened between them had nothing to do with satin sheets or dingy motels. At seven, three mornings a week, Adrianna came in to work at Foodland, and from the second morning already, she found herself transfixed at the kind of attention Stuart paid to his lettuce, his potatoes, and his citrus. He'd lay the garden produce in order one piece at a time, taking care that each apple was polished with the bottom of his green Foodland apron.

Once the kids were all in school a block away, business slumped for about an hour before the housewives started coming in with long lists. During that hour, Adrianna watched this man's hands nurture his goods. She'd stand in an empty aisle with the price gun, slapping red tags on cans of pie filling she emptied from a box, then stop, and from the corner of her eye she'd watch Stuart arranging bananas against the green mat on the fruit counter—picking them up gently, inspecting them, then laying them in horizontal waves, stepping back occasionally to be sure of the arrangement he'd set. Stuart Mackey was a man who loved with his hands. Adrianna had shopped at his store for years herself, but only once she started working there did she notice something in this man whom she'd known her entire life—sincerity and grace, two attributes sadly lacking in her own husband of twenty-three years.

But Stuart's Foodland, like Les's business, was doomed to failure. The new SuperMart at the edge of town was slowly destroying a family business of more than seventy years. Stuart could not match their prices. He simply lacked the resources to advertise the way they did (four full pages in the *Shopper,* double off for any coupons any day of the week), and he couldn't stay open all hours.

He'd lost his wife, Beth, to cancer five years before in one of those incredible stories people have trouble believing even when they stand at the graveside. She'd been feeling run down, she said, so she went to Dr. Howells, who scheduled tests immediately. They opened her up, took one look, and shook their heads. In two months, she was gone. Stuart was alone.

What grew between Stuart and Adrianna Meekhof was nurtured by quiet conversation that grew in familiarity and intimacy each morning at about nine, when the store was otherwise quiet. It was intimate and loving conversation, with something always left unsaid—their mutual need. Sometimes at night Adrianna fell asleep alone dreaming of Stuart beside her, her own husband out somewhere trying frantically to hold on to his insulation business.

Both Stuart and Adrianna understood what was happening, and for a long time they quietly resisted, never speaking of what both of them felt. But the sixth anniversary of Beth Mackey's death very subtly changed everything. These are good people, I want you to know, but sufferers, both of them. And they found something in each other that they recognized was painfully lacking in their own lives, something that, according to Adrianna, became undeniable one May 14.

There's a bell attached to Foodland's front door, has been for years. It's a museum piece, something that reminds people of a time when making the store a going concern didn't require crowded aisles sixteen hours a day. Stuart was there when Adrianna came in—he opens at six. Early in the morning he is very quiet, but then he is never loud. But that morning she didn't have to be told why he seemed distant. She knew very well.

"I'm sorry," she said as she gathered the strings of her own apron and tied them behind her back.

Stuart determinedly grinned.

There was a delivery man in the store, a young guy in a uniform, Larry, who stocks potato chips and pretzels.

"Ever since Sunday I've been gearing up for it," Stuart told her. He was sitting behind the desk in the back, looking over the books. "It's like chemo," he said, "you find yourself obsessed with it long before it gets into your veins, and you make yourself sick with anticipation. You know, if I could just not look at a calendar, I'd be okay," he said. "Maybe if I thought of this day as June 14, it would be just another day at work."

Adrianna had long ago learned that often the most compassionate way of dealing with people who hurt is silence.

"Sometimes I still get angry about it," he said, "about her leaving that way. Here I sit in the back of the store and I don't have a dime's worth of desire to go up front or anything. I don't give a hang about anything. I don't want to talk," he told her. "I don't want to see anyone. I just want to sit back here and mope."

"I can handle the front," she told him.

"That's not the point," he said. "The point is it's six years already and I'm still mad about it."

"You're not mad at her," she said.

"Of course not," he told her.

She reached up above the blackboard for the marking pens. The work schedule is drawn up there. "Hey," she said, picking up the eraser, "you're right. It's June 14—look," and she erased the word "May" and wrote in "June."

He smiled, swung around on the stool. He was grateful. It was just a little thing she'd done, but it was a good thing. He looked at her closely, and he asked a question that connected them to a whole world of love and sin. "Would you like me to forget?" he said, knowing it was a daring question.

It's early, quiet in the store. She breathed once or twice, waiting, then, "I just don't want you to hurt so bad," she said.

He knew it was a skillfully drawn answer, and he dropped his eyes to his hands. "I spent what—forty years, forty-two years— of my life thinking May 14 was nothing more than May 14. Now it's like the *only* day. Ade," he said, "I forgot our anniversary twice, you know—and she never let me forget it either. But now the only day of the whole year I can't forget is May 14."

Adrianna wanted something else out of this, so she looked at him pleadingly. "I lied," she said. "Today *is* May 14."

He put his hands down at the edge of the desk. "Am I *supposed* to forget?" he asked. "Is that the way it works—eventually people simply forget everything they ever loved? I mean, does it say in the Bible somewhere that it's all just going to slip away?"

"Would you want it to?"

"It hurts," he said.

"Because you loved her," she told him.

137

"Because I loved her more than anything—"

"Then why forget?" she said.

Adrianna was little more than an arm's length away, but he didn't fully understand exactly what she felt when he said right then, "If I didn't care so very, very much about her, it wouldn't be so awful. If I didn't love her so much, and she didn't love me," he said, "it wouldn't be so bad."

At that point, she couldn't hold herself back, so she told him what was coming up from her heart at that very moment with all of his talk of so much love. "Maybe *you're* the lucky one," she said, and she picked up the feather duster, turned, and walked past the already opened cartons of cereal boxes, embarrassed at letting go that way. "I can handle the front," she said at the swinging doors. "You stay back here."

"Ade," he said, "I'm sorry."

"You don't have to be," she told him. But all the way to the front she fought tears, not so much for her marriage, not even for Stuart, but for her own weakness. How could she have said that? What right did she have to inflict her own hurt on him— *this* morning, his horrible anniversary? It was wrong, plain wrong, *sin* wrong. There she was, throwing her own pain in the path of his healing. She remembered not hearing the bell— there were no customers—so immediately she straightened her shoulders, turned around up near the front, and headed back to the office. "I shouldn't have said that," she told Stuart. "I had no right. It was out of place, imposing myself on you."

He came off the stool and held her for the first time, simply held her, the two of them in each other's arms when they heard the squeaking wheels of Larry's hand truck, a warning that stopped Stuart from saying what he had at the tip of his tongue.

The anniversary of the death of Beth Mackey occasioned the first moment the two of them opened up to each other's pain.

What Adrianna knew already that morning when she'd tripped on her own hurt while trying to help him stumble along through his own was that purposefully stepping away from each other would take time and more pain. So this love affair continued, both of them conscious of each other every quiet minute they worked side by side, while they steadfastly avoided running up the tally on what they thought to be their mutual sin.

What Adrianna saw in the way Stuart handled produce—bunches of grapes, a shipment of grapefruit, a whole section of oranges—was graciousness. And when he held her in his arms, which happened more and more often, she felt immensely treasured.

Both of them in their late-forties, they fell in love despite their better judgment. And yet they saw each other only in Foodland, only three mornings a week, both of them wearing bright green aprons tied in a tight bow at the back. As long as their love remained unconsummated, as long as they lived in the shadowy world of unacknowledged need, as long as their mutual sense of righteousness restrained them from following the lead of their emotions, as long as they prayed together in the back of the store, their desire only grew.

October 27. The front door of Foodland had a ridge of frost near the bottom for the first morning since last winter. The front windows were plastered with life-sized cardboard figures—witches aboard long broomsticks, scrambling ghosts and goblins, and a huge yellow moon smiling toothlessly. There were enough pumpkins lined up along the floor to remind Stuart he'd probably overstocked.

Adrianna sat on the sloping skirt of the counter up front. Somewhere in the store, a few customers sought out milk or bread or cereal. Stuart dropped candy down the chutes of a wire display. The two of them had been talking up front more often because they knew it was safer, and today they were talking about football, about Mark, Adrianna's son, who always makes the big plays—and had again the previous Friday night, as the middle linebacker.

"He would never have gone out, I think," Adrianna said, "if it hadn't been for the pressure."

"From the coaches?" Stuart asked.

"Hildebrand made it known when he was a sophomore that if Mark came out he'd probably be starting. He's built like his father," she said. "You can't believe the way he eats."

"You'd rather not have him play?"

"When he got into high school I was scared. It's so dangerous. And he didn't argue. I think he was happy to be able to say his mother didn't want him playing."

"Now he's fierce, some people say."

Adrianna looked up the aisle to see if one of the customers was coming. "Sometimes you don't recognize your own kid, I guess," she said. "I don't know where he gets it. His father used to take him fishing. I swear, he hated it—couldn't stand it when his father would take a bullhead off the hook."

"All kids go through that," Stuart said.

"Then why don't they stay that way?" she asked.

He leaned down and sorted through the candy rack. "They grow up," he told her.

"If it were up to me, I still wouldn't let him play," she said.

"What does Les say?" Stuart asked her.

She hated to hear her husband's name on his lips, hated to hear it at all in the store. So when she talked about him, what she said came out angrily. "It busts his buttons to see Mark do so well. He wears this pin all over—it's got Mark's picture on it and it's supposed to be for his mom." She pulls up her nose. "In a way, Mark's the star his father never was."

Stuart looked over at her as if there were not enough of her to satisfy everything in him that was starving, and when she saw his eyes that way, their own talking little more than a distraction to what they felt, she thought that just to be beside

140

him in moments like that, just to have him next to her in those long morning silences, was enough to warm her into life. Maybe, she told herself, that's all she needed of him. But then it seemed so one-sided, as if she were using him. "Thanks," she said, because she wanted him to know so much that she couldn't say.

Stuart broke the uneasy silence and walked to the front windows, windows full of witches, and as he passed her he simply touched her shoulder, just laid a hand there, not at all to be forward, only in love. Ten minutes later, the store empty, the two of them found their way to the back again, the place they tried so hard to avoid, where they locked themselves up in each other's arms, oblivious to almost everything but the old bell up front.

Adrianna could have said that her husband never really learned to love her at all, but she never did say that, not to Stuart, not to me, not to anyone, not even a whisper of it to herself—which is not to say she didn't wholeheartedly believe it. As far as I know, Adrianna never blamed her husband for what she did.

But Stuart Mackey shattered Adrianna's resolve with his hands, and that's why she finally announced to both men in her life that she had to quit her part-time job at Foodland. Stuart offered to stay in the back of the store and do the books or handle ordering, said he'd never wander up front through those quiet morning hours; but the offer was futile and he knew it—because he knew Adrianna. He'd grown to love her for the very strength that bound her to her husband and made her walking out the store forever absolutely necessary.

Adrianna's son, Mark, was gone the night she told Les. He was out with his girlfriend somewhere. It was not yet ten. Les was reading a church paper—the man went to church regularly.

141

His father was the great preacher, after all. But I'm not at all sure what he actually heard at church, even though he had been going his whole life. That night, Adrianna said his feet were up on the matching hassock of a chair his mother had reupholstered for them, like they always were when he was home.

"I'm not going in tomorrow," she told him. "Today I quit."

"Got a better offer?" He never dropped the paper he was reading.

"I can find something," she told him. She had a book in front of her, opened almost halfway. "I'm tired of it," she said.

Whatever honesty had existed between them had disappeared into the cold, years before.

"He doesn't pay enough?" Les said.

"I want to find something with people," she replied. "Most of the time all I do is stamp coffee cans."

He dropped the newspaper. "I wish I could hire you myself," he said. He leaned his head back against the top of the chair. "I wish I had something for you—anything."

"It's not going well?" she asked.

"I got some buttons I can push yet," he said. "I'm not quite dead." Credit him with looking at her then, because he did. He slipped his reading glasses off and laid his head back again. "Stuart's got to be about the best guy in the world to work for," he said. "Ain't a better soul around. That's why his business is dying."

"He's treated me well."

"Probably too good," Les said, twirling the glasses. "He's going down, you know. That store doesn't stand a chance, not with everybody going to SuperMart. Too bad though."

"He didn't fire me," she said. "He never said a word about not being able to keep me on."

"Someday he's going to have to read the score," Les told her. "What's a guy like that going to do once his business is gone, Ade?" he said. "Poor guy. Got no wife."

Everything inside her wanted to tell him the truth, but restraint offered such safety that unburdening herself was really unthinkable.

"Not very busy, I suppose, early in the morning," he said, putting down the glasses and jarring a cigarette out of the pack beside him on the table. "You could ask him to give you another shift—but then you couldn't get supper going." He turned that cigarette in his fingers. "How about at night?"

"Stuart's not open at night."

"Ought to be—if he's going to keep his business. Maybe you should tell him."

She pulled her legs beneath her. "I think he'd rather go under."

"Well, he's going to."

She watched him tap the end of the cigarette against the face of his watch. "He was telling me the other day about the Netherlands," she said. "You know, there's a law there that all shops close at five. It's actually a *law*," she said. "Everything shuts down at five o'clock so that a small businessman can keep some family life. Can you believe that?"

"Socialism," he said, toying with that cigarette. "So what you got in mind?" he asked. "You could always be an aide at school or something. More people stuff, that's what you want?"

"I don't know," she said.

"I never heard you complain before," he said, taking that cigarette and placing it in the corner of his lips. "Now that I think about it, I'm surprised you're throwing in the towel." Finally, he pulled himself up in the chair and looked at her strangely. "What's bugging you?" he said quickly, exhaling smoke. "There's more to this."

She felt the look that nearly broke her, the way he turned his face, the old angles like shards of glass.

"You aren't telling me something," he said. He puffed again on his cigarette, blew smoke out the corner of his lips. "You never said a thing before."

And then, just as sharply, she said, "You never asked."

With that retort, something of a slap, they both crossed a line.

He raised his eyebrows and waited, thinking. Then, oddly, he laughed. "You're too old for an affair," he said.

She could feel a fist close tightly in her chest. "That's why I'm quitting," she told him, then put her feet on the floor and left the room. She walked into the kitchen and stood over the sink, staring out at the neighbor's driveway, nausea rising.

Les had many faults, but he was neither stupid nor naive. He knew very well that something between the two of them had long ago perished. The blunt facts of his own failures were as obvious as they were instantaneously humiliating. So he went after her, swearing, sensing blood. "Isn't it enough that all around you your husband's business is going belly-up? Now this too?"

She felt the man fill the room with his powerful physical presence.

"What's going on?" he demanded. "You messing around with that guy? Good night, Ade, you're a grandma!"

"I told you," she said. "I quit for that reason."

"Why?"

"You said it," she told him.

"Because you had an affair?"

"Because I'm not going to."

"Does that mean you *did,* Ade? What is it? I'm your husband. Did you? I demand to know."

"What?" she said, turning toward him. "What exactly do you want to know?"

What he screamed at her included a word that hadn't been used in their house in all their years together, and it hit her with so much grief that she turned quickly, viciously. "My goodness, Les," she screamed, "how can you be so foul?"

"Don't call *me* foul—what about you and the holy grocer? What do you call what you did?"

"We didn't—"

"My goodness—a *grandma,* and you commit adultery like some on-fire kid? In the old days people like you had to stand up in front of church and confess—maybe I ought to make you do that. Maybe I ought to take you to the preacher right now." He turned his wrath on Stuart. "It's his fault, wasn't it? Being without a wife that long. He's the one that came on—the righteous grocer with his hands on all the help. That pervert."

"Shut up!" she shouted.

"Where?" he said. "In the store?" He threw the cigarette on the floor and stomped on it.

"Never," she said.

"What do you mean, *never?* I won't hear *never.* I won't believe it, Ade. I won't believe *never* or it wouldn't lead to this."

"It didn't happen!" she said.

"I know men," he said, "so don't tell me something I know better."

"Shut up," she said.

"Admit it!"

"Never."

"You liar," he said. "You and him—good grief, Ade, you call yourself a Christian?"

And with that, she hit him so hard across the face that his head jerked sideways and he had to step back to keep his balance. He held his hand up to his jaw and looked at her, his face full of rage. She said she saw eyes that seemed emptied of soul, so white and shiny that for the moment he seemed to have lost altogether the image of God.

That was the last time she saw him alive.

Angry, jealous, hurt, Les Meekhof left home just a few minutes later, consumed with hate and stunned by shock. He did exactly what most people here would have expected of him—he drove to Stuart's house.

Stuart's old house has a long driveway, long enough to require a tractor and loader when the snow falls. It took Les thirty seconds, at most, to drive up to the back of the house, another fifteen seconds to get to the back door. It was another twenty or so before Stuart put down the newspaper, swung his legs off the ottoman, and stood, not quickly, yawning as if to show some innocence. Finally he walked through the dining room and into the kitchen to the back door. He had, at most, two minutes to come up with a story.

"Mr. Mackey," Les said, his hat in his hand like a kindly visitor. "I got business. It's about Ade. Seems to me you owe me an explanation."

Stuart lacked sufficient guile to dance for him. "What did she tell you?" he asked.

"She told me you fired her for incompetence," Les said.

"Incompetence?" Stuart said.

"That's right. She said you told her that she rang up too many prices incorrectly. She said you told her that it was costing you too much money to have to cover for her all the time."

Stuart raised a hand. "Come in," he said. "Sit down here."

Les never unbuttoned his coat. He took a chair from the table and laid his hat in front of him, knowing he already had Stuart Mackey on the ropes.

"You want some coffee?" Stuart asked.

Les glanced down at his watch. "No. Keeps me awake."

Stuart went to the stove as if he hadn't even heard the response. "You don't mind if I do?" he said. "Maybe I can make you tea?"

"Don't bother," Les said. "Look, I'm here as my wife's husband and a businessman. I'm here to tell you that the least you can do is be honest with her. Don't blame her for your problems. Everybody knows you're having trouble keeping up nowadays."

"That's not it," Stuart said.

146

But Les kept on turning the knife. "My wife doesn't have the greatest self-image," he said. "And I can believe that she doesn't always get every penny straight—I've lived with her for twenty-five years." He was toying with Stuart, looking to hang him with his own words. "But I'm disappointed in you because you hurt her when the fact is that you can't take the truth."

"The truth?"

"The truth is you can't compete with SuperMart, and everybody knows it."

Stuart's mind went blank.

"You can fire her," Les told him. "That's all right with me because I like her home." He crossed his arms over his chest. "But what bugs me is that my wife is sitting home right now bawling."

"You want a Coke?" Stuart asked.

"I'll take a Coke," Les told him. "Like I said, I can believe that she messed up—I've lived with her for all these years, after all. Let me tell you, when she went that first day off to your store, she was scared to death. It was like seeing your first child off to kindergarten."

Stuart reached in the fridge for a Coke. "You want a glass?" he said.

Les reached for the can. "I'm scared that it's going to take a lot more now to get her out again. I'm sorry you lost your wife and all, Stu," he said, "but sometimes living with a woman who's a tangle of nerves is something else. She can be such a mess."

Stuart couldn't live with the direction this was going, as Les had to know he couldn't. Stuart saw himself to blame for falling for a married woman. He is not a man who lies easily. "I didn't fire her for incompetence," Stuart said, standing just behind Les.

"You can't tell me my Ade's a liar," Les told him. "I won't believe that. That woman can't lie."

147

"That's true," Stuart said, backing away toward the counter behind him.

"What are you saying?" Les asked.

Stuart Mackey is not a liar, but at that moment he followed the path he believed this woman he loved had taken, and he too resorted to deceit, simply to protect her. "The truth is," he said, "I came on to her—and she's lying to protect me. That's the truth," he told Les. "She's not taking the blame for what I did."

Les swore, as if it were the first time he'd heard the truth.

"I'm everything you call me," Stuart claimed. "I'm sorry. You want to hit me—go ahead. It'd probably feel as good for me as it would for you."

"I don't want to hurt my hand," Les said. "So what did you do?"

"I told you," Stuart said.

"I want to know *exactly*," Les responded. "We're talking about my wife here."

"What do you mean?"

"I want to know exactly what you did to her."

Stuart stared at his hands. "I don't know what came over me—I swear it," he said. "She was in the back of the store—about a week ago now." He reached for words. "She was just standing there, and I just went for her—" He stumbled, shook. "I don't know how to describe it. She was putting on her apron, tying the strings behind her back, and I wanted to touch her—"

"You pervert," Les sputtered. "You put your hands on my wife?"

"Yes," he said—and for the first time he could speak the truth. "I did, and I'm sorry."

The low rumble of the coffeemaker slowed. Stuart took a cup from the cupboard.

"You ought to see a doctor," Les said. He was enjoying himself, turning the knife artfully with what he already knew. "You're sick," he said to Stuart. "You need a shrink."

148

"Maybe I do. Maybe you're right on that one, Les."

"So what'd she do?"

Stuart's hands went so tight the cup shook in his hands. "She pulled away," he said. "She started crying right away."

"That's the whole story?" Les demanded. "Once? Just one time in the back of the store, you grabbed her?"

Stuart inferred that what he'd already said wasn't enough. "Four times," he said, "maybe five." He put down the cup and poured a cup from the pot. He started to turn toward the table when, completely unexpectedly, he caught the back of Les's hand so hard across his face that the hot coffee flew over the wall.

Had he even an ounce of violence in him, Stuart Mackey would have likely swallowed it at that moment anyway; but he doesn't. He gathered himself on the floor and got to a knee. "I'm sorry," he said, looking up. "I got it coming."

What Les did at that moment cannot really be described as a kick. It wasn't a kick. What Les did right then with his right foot was jam Stuart, stomp him as if he were kick-starting a motorcycle. He stuck a foot on Stuart's shoulder and shoved so that Stuart, still on his knees, rolled backward into the wastebasket across the room, a tangle of arms and legs. If Les had leaned back and flung his huge foot, he could have broken Stuart's ribs. But he held back, and Stuart knew it.

Why? We can only conjecture. This is what I want to believe: What Les Meekhof realized in Stuart Mackey's unflinching acceptance of whatever humiliation Les could inflict was a depth of feeling for a woman he himself hadn't loved that completely in twenty years. What he knew at that moment was not that life or God had dealt him continuously bad hands, but that in business as well as at home he had played whatever cards he'd ever held dead wrong.

No one knows exactly what happened, but given the circumstances of that awful night, we can guess—and I think we should. When Les left, he drove that pickup into that big shed, took out one of the long tubes used to blow in insulation, fixed it to the truck window, and let that truck idle. No longer was his hate aimed at his wife or Stuart Mackey. The rage likely turned suddenly inward, hate zeroing in on his own heart with the tenacity of a turned-down divining rod.

Two hours passed. It was just after ten. Adrianna says she was in no frame of mind to sleep. She had an idea where Les had gone, but she was afraid to call Stuart Mackey. At ten, she watched the news. The windows were open to the warmest Halloween on record in Barneveld. The backyard trees rushed with the heaves of a wet southern wind. Windows creaked. The back door rattled on its hinges. Alone in the house, she heard every last motion.

What was forming in her mind was an argument she'd been having with God ever since she'd begun to work at Foodland: How was it possible that continuing to live with this man could be right, when it sometimes seemed worse than death? Must the price of righteousness be happiness?

At eleven, with nowhere else to turn, she called Stuart, who told her what had happened at his house. They both knew, then, that the real truth had to be told.

"I parked up the road," Stuart told her when she let him in the door. "I figured he'd better not see my car when he comes home."

They refused to embrace. She saw his swollen lip, but he waved away her attention. They decided the two of them should try to hunt Les down, and the first place they looked was the shop, the biggest steel shed ever in Barneveld. They found him in the pickup, his face cherry red and his soul already departed.

It's quite impossible to enter the mind of Adrianna at that

moment, for what was there was as shattered as the promises she and Les had long ago made to each other. She sat on a folding chair while Stuart scrambled to save her husband. He took Les behind the shoulders and dragged him from the truck. First, he laid him on the cement and did what he could to salve his own guilt, even mouth-to-mouth.

Does it matter whose idea it was to disguise what happened? Do we need so badly to affix blame for the lie these two good people created that night? When he conceded to what he knew was true, and with Ade's consent, Stuart pulled Les Meekhof's body across the floor and through the door to the little office space in the back. He slumped the body over a desk full of bills, raised both hands, and pulled a pen from the drawer; then he placed it in Les's fingers. Together, Stuart and Adrianna waited again, this time for the shiny redness to disappear from the body. Then they called for help.

The ambulance crew, on seeing Les, conceded to Stuart's prognosis—the man was dead of a heart attack. Doc Howells himself was called from his bed and found Les slumped over the desk, the very man Howells had warned just two weeks before to stop smoking, to lay off booze, to avoid stress, to lose weight. When Doc wrote out the report, he thought again how, forty years before, he should have decided to go into veterinary medicine because people treat their hogs better than they do themselves. There was no need for toxicology, he figured, so he never drew blood.

It was a big funeral, well attended, even though in his life it would have been possible to count Les's real friends on one hand. I knew nothing at the time except that Les had never really found a business that would work, nor had he found, perhaps, himself. I knew nothing of the suicide, nor anything of what had led to his death, so I talked to Adrianna and her son, Mark, about hope and peace. The Lord didn't so much as give me the words to say, as talked to her himself in the words of Isaiah 40:

> The LORD is the everlasting God,
>> the Creator of the ends of the earth.
> He will not grow tired or weary,
>> and his understanding no one can fathom.
> He gives strength to the weary
>> and increases the power of the weak.
> Even youths grow tired and weary,
>> and young men stumble and fall;
> but those who hope in the LORD
>> will renew their strength.
> They will soar on wings like eagles;
>> they will run and not grow weary,
>> they will walk and not be faint (NIV).

People came to the funeral not so much to honor the deceased as to comfort the living. Adrianna was broken, her grief a testimony, people thought, to the long-suffering journey she must have taken with a man most thought unlovable. Some claimed that to see her weep the way she did gave others courage to see themselves through situations that sometimes looked as hopeless.

For three days Adrianna cried. And all the time, Stuart was there with her. No one thought his constant presence at all suspicious, knowing his character—and hers—and understanding how it was they had come to know each other in the year Adrianna had worked mornings at Foodland. Besides, Stuart had lost a spouse himself and understood exactly the specific pain she suffered.

In fact, when they married six months later, only the most gossipy ever entertained the possibility of something otherwise plotted. Everyone smiled. They were two wonderful people, after all—the very picture of devotion. Some of us at Barneveld

Calvary even claimed that the whole story was itself a parable of God's love, since a happy new life with Stuart Mackey seemed almost a reward for all Adrianna Meekhof's years with her first husband. No one—no woman certainly—had ever envied her, not even when the insulation business was booming.

When the lights were finally turned out in the shop the night Les took his own life, after the EMTs were gone, after Stuart had taken Adrianna home and told Mark what had happened to his father, after Doc Howells put the finishing touches on the paperwork, one item remained undiscovered.

Perhaps what happened will bring hope to those who consider what Les Meekhof did worthy of eternal suffering, because before he picked out the flexible tube, before he'd plugged the gap left in the window with rags from the barrel, before he'd even turned on the engine in that Dodge Ram, he sat at the desk where the entire town thought he'd died, and wrote a note to his son.

Something of what has happened to me, Les must have thought, needs to make some sense. Maybe it was his father's legacy, his father the preacher. What Les said was this, in a nutshell: "I've done it all wrong, Mark. Don't make my mistakes."

I've read the note myself.

Les affixed a stamp to a windowed envelope, wrote Mark's name and his own address above the cellophane, and delivered it to the business mailbox out on the street, setting up the signal flag for the postman before he walked back to the shop for the last time.

The mailman thought it odd that an envelope from Meekhof Insulation would be in Les's family mail, but he stuck it in the box, as required by law, and never really gave it another thought—not even after he'd heard of Les's sudden heart attack and untimely death.

It was only a day after Les's death, and Adrianna was crying in the family room when Mark came in from the porch with the mail. He threw the other things on the table and went upstairs to read whatever it was his father had written to him alone.

Mark knew right then what had really happened, even if he didn't know exactly why.

Mark, who'd been a standout linebacker, received a college scholarship that spring, even though he'd not distinguished himself on the football field after the sudden death of his father, an event that obviously robbed him of some of his viciousness. A college in suburban Chicago gambled on Mark's recovery from grief—besides, he was a fine student. But after a year at college, Mark quit football altogether.

He gave it up when he found Jesus and gave himself to where his heavenly Father would lead. That calling became the ministry—just like his fabled grandfather. All of Barneveld was proud.

He fell in love with a girl named Sara, and on the night he became engaged he told her what he knew about his father's suicide, a word he never used himself. She insisted that they see a pastor somewhere, so they came to me.

Five years after Les Meekhof's death, the truth seeped out in my office, and what I advised Mark to do, someday, when the time was right, was to approach his mother with what he knew and simply tell her everything. "You really can't live with a lie," I told him. I didn't know if I could either.

Not long after, Mark called me and told me he wanted me there when the whole truth came out. So I went. I sat there in the Meekhof family home, Adrianna and Stuart on the couch, Mark across from them in a stiff hardwood chair, Sara's arm around his as she sat beside him in a folding chair. I didn't say much at all. No one did. Mark handed his mother the letter, and immediately she cried. Stuart, this time, didn't try to comfort her because, I assume, he knew that in this secret he was an accomplice.

No one attempted any explanation. Neither of them tried to excuse what he or she had done. They told Mark what had happened in Foodland, how the two of them had parted rather than go on into something both knew they would regret. So all that was expressed that night was sorrow, perhaps a sorrow left unexpressed at the funeral. If moments like that can be said to be beautiful, then that night will live in my mind as a masterpiece, love all around.

I left there that night holding a secret I knew I wouldn't tell, for how should it be known? A newspaper article? An announcement in the church bulletin? There was no way the facts of the story could represent the human loss that had already occurred.

Mr. and Mrs. Mackey have lived happily, but not always comfortably; they share a lie, after all, as do I.

But I can find motives as long as your arm to excuse the deception. They'd quit their relationship honorably, never having consummated anything. Adrianna had resigned her job for all the best reasons. Les had treated them both with contempt. Their lie even lent some honor, at least, to the name of Les Meekhof—and to the old preacher's family.

So why am I telling this now? Perhaps because I still believe the old text about the truth and its ability to make us free. What we all need to hear is the whole story, with all its dark corners, because even here, amid our sin, and because of it, there is beauty. Our God reigns.

Maybe what's most amazing about the joys and concerns at Barneveld Calvary is not that the secrets exist, but that those who know them are able to live with them, just as all of us do.

Ted Bennink and the King of the Jews

Theodore George Bennink

Theodore "Ted" Bennink died Tuesday night in his sleep of a heart attack he suffered at home. He was seventy-two years old. He is survived by his loving wife, Katharine; his stepson, Art, of Riverside, California; his daughter, Marie, of Bellflower, California; his son, Dr. Mark, of Des Moines; his ten grandchildren and two great-grandchildren.

Mr. Bennink was born April 26, 1918, to Pete and Ella Bennink, who lived six miles north of Barneveld. He was preceded in death by his parents, two brothers, and three sisters. Before World War II, he worked on his father's farm. When he returned from three years of service in Europe wounded, he became a shoe repairman and the owner of Ted's Shoes, a Main Street business in Barneveld for many years. He retired in 1983.

Mr. Bennink was a member of Calvary Church, Barneveld, where he served God's people faithfully for many years as an elder. He is remembered by his family as a kind man, a loving father, and a dedicated follower of Jesus Christ our Lord. His life was a wonderful witness to the love of God. Blessed to the Lord are the lives of his saints.

There is no reason to read the funeral arrangements, since Mr. Bennink was dutifully committed to the earth from which he came more than a year ago already. His children have long ago returned to their homes and lives, and his widow is visited almost daily by many loving friends who know her grief. When she wakes in the morning, she has already begun to remember that the man she married so long ago is no longer a room away, sitting alone at the kitchen table over an open Bible, his daily ritual for all those years they lived together happily as husband and wife.

He's the last of the Benninks in Barneveld, so it's likely even his name will be forgotten soon enough, although it is engraved on a bronze plaque set in the ground beneath a 75 mm howitzer the city picked up for shipping costs from the army following the war—a battle gun that had never made it out of the country, in fact. Only old folks remember Ted Bennink's name, even today. "The man with the big broom beard," someone younger might say, "who owned the shoe store."

Long ago, Ted stuck a buffalo nickel to the countertop, laid it down there with the toughest glue he could find. Generations of Barneveld kids tried to grab that nickel when he wasn't looking, but they never got it, of course. Even though the shop's been sold already for several years, that buffalo nickel is still there and it still won't move.

"First Lieutenant Ted Bennink" the plaque in the park says, directly beneath the name of Private Charles Attema, the man whose wife Ted married five years after Private Attema died in the war that wounded Mr. Bennink. Not once in Ted's life did he even glance at the plaque across the road from his shoe shop, even though he'd seen the howitzer out of the corner of his eye at least once a day from the broad front window of the store. He avoided that plaque, just as he avoided thinking about the war—not anxiously but deliberately, with the same ritual deliberateness with which he'd written out his life's daily pattern of personal morning devotions, a practice he had picked up in the war, like so much else he forever carried with him.

He never looked at that bronze plaque, never saw his name in gold—never wanted to—because when the war was over, when Ted was back home again, his hip in constant pain from the bullets he'd taken, he alone knew very well that he was no more a first lieutenant than was Private Attema, the man whose wife he'd begun to court. That plaque does not tell the truth, and therein lies the story of Ted Bennink, a story from Barneveld Calvary that should be told and must be remembered.

Little Bighorn is a place on the prairie so featureless it is difficult to imagine something as significant as Custer's Last Stand could have happened there. On a moody, cloudy day, one has trouble discerning earth from sky. Here and there, occasional ragged clumps of trees saunter up to the bank of the Little Bighorn River and sprout on the face of the land like unruly sideburns. Some of Custer's men, facing inevitable death, tried to run or ride to cover in those patchy groves. Some even made it, but they died anyway, flushed like rabbits from a thicket. Just outside of those clumps of trees, the men who cleaned up in the wake of the battle found bodies that looked like porcupines, a grotesque bouquet of arrows blossoming from their chests.

Ted Bennink was there in 1968, when his son, Mark, then only sixteen, made it very clear that as long as they were in the Black Hills for their annual vacation, he and his father really should go a ways farther west and actually see the battlefield he'd read so much about.

Even as a child, Ted had envisioned Little Bighorn as more mountainous than it is, the battlefield itself more secret, hidden. But once he got there, he realized that no soldier could hide very long at the Little Bighorn. Ted and his son stood on a blacktop walk and surveyed the very spot where nearly a century before, hundreds of troops under Custer's command were slaughtered. Ted had little interest in war of any kind. Mark, as always, jabbered.

"You can go through here with one of those metal detectors, and you still find bullets," Mark said, "only it's illegal now. It would have to be or everybody'd do it. Shoot, I would. Wouldn't that be great? You find this buckle or something, maybe one of those metal insignias all those cavalry guys wore on their hats."

159

"You're thinking of the Civil War," Ted said.

"No, I'm not. You've seen them on TV."

"This isn't TV," Ted told his son.

"I know, but they had those insignias—two crossed swords. Right up here," he pointed to his forehead. "You can buy them in the Visitor Center."

"Replicas," Ted said.

"Of course," Mark replied, "but what I'm saying is, wouldn't it be great to take a metal detector out here and really find something like that—something right from the battle?"

Mark was a model student, a basketball star, junior class president, and such a fine athlete that just six months after that trip to Little Bighorn he got a scholarship to Drake University. The coach told him that even if he couldn't dribble, the university would have given him a full ride. That's the kind of kid he was. Today he teaches at Drake—history, in fact. After his father's funeral, he told me this story, a fragment of a mystery he'd never quite understood.

"They still don't know why Custer attacked when he did," Mark told his father, although the information wasn't meant necessarily for Ted. It was a lecture that just spilled out of Mark, even though he still had a year of high school ahead of him. "It really made no sense," he said. "The whole encampment was much bigger than anything any 'white eyes' had ever seen."

"White eyes?" Ted said, chuckling.

"Some people figure he didn't have a clue as to how many Indians there really were." All during this commentary, Mark never really looked at Ted. He was just talking, and that's what drew a crowd of other tourists, who lined up and listened in as if Mark were the tour guide. "Some people think that once Custer attacked the village, he realized it was like trying to take on a whole city. But he didn't know until he started firing." Mark shook his head. "How d'you like that, Dad? You ride in

160

thinking you're going to scare up the local hostiles and it's really something huge—like the Los Angeles of Indians."

"He was cocky, wasn't he?" some guy asked, a man holding an unruly child while trying to light a cigarette. "He did it because he was chasing down glory, wasn't he?"

Mark never batted an eye. "He was cocky, I guess—at least from what you read."

The man tumbled the child into his left arm and straightened out his T-shirt. "I always thought he was cocky. I always thought it was just a full-blown case of cockiness," the guy said. "And he had a white horse, didn't he?" the man continued. "Think of that out here—a white horse! Geez, you're just asking to take bullets." He flipped his hand around toward the open fields as if there were nothing at all around him. "Look at this! What would make a man want a white stallion in a godforsaken place like this?" He laughed in outright disbelief. The child was scrambling, almost out of control. "Why don't you sit still and learn something for once?" the man said to the child.

They were bothered by the man, Mark said, so they started to walk back to the car. But Mark couldn't really loosen himself from the grip of the place. "I don't think anybody knows for sure whether he rode a white horse," he told his father. "Some people believe everything they read."

In the air was the fresh smell of cut grass. They'd seen lawn mowers all over, men in park shirts keeping everything up, the whole place picture-perfect, just like it once was. "They want to keep all this just like it was a hundred years ago," Ted told him.

Mark told me he didn't understand right away what was going on in his father's head.

The ranger had claimed that the actual trees that once stood in clumps along the Little Bighorn were completely gone now, but what had grown in their place made the whole area look quite similar to what they might have seen nearly a century before. "When you stand out there at the viewpoint overlooking the main battlefield, just imagine that what you're seeing isn't much different from what any cavalryman would have seen when he came up on this place ninety years ago," the ranger said. Mark soaked it all in. "Other than thousands of Indian tepees, that is, the place looks very, very similar."

What Ted was remembering right then were those French towns, the Belgian villages, the German countryside—most of Europe had already been destroyed by the time his unit was chasing Krauts across Europe. Nothing there could possibly look the same, nothing at all. Everything would be different. It would all be gone—every sign of what had been there.

"You know," Mark told his dad, "I always thought they died in a tight little clump or something—like 'circle up the wagons,' you know? I thought they all died together, but they didn't. It was much worse than that, man."

"How do you know so much?" Ted said.

"Read it," Mark said, without really thinking. "Maybe it would have been nice, you know—I mean, if they'd all died together." He raised his eyebrows. "Maybe it would have been easier."

"Maybe," Ted said. "How come you want to know about all of this?"

Mark jerked his head backward quickly. "You guys like me to read," he said offhandedly. "But you want to know what really gets me?" He stopped, folded his arms across his chest, looked at his father closely, and then said something Mark the history professor confessed it was difficult for him to repeat, even years later. "After it was over and they were all dead," he told his father, "the Sioux squaws came up—and the kids too," he said. He stood there for a minute, then laughed as if to cover something he wasn't proud of, but something that was, nonetheless, on his mind. He was only a kid.

"So what?" his father told him. "What are you saying?"

"They, like, finished the job, Dad," he said.

"I don't get it."

"I mean, the ones who weren't dead—the women killed them. Sometimes they bashed their faces with clubs so hard that the men couldn't even be identified."

"What do you mean, Mark?" Ted asked.

"The women, Dad—and the kids." He threw up his hands as if nothing more could be said. "They sliced up Custer's men—the women did. Cut off their arms and heads. Even other parts, Dad." He shook his head and shut his eyes as if the thought alone had blinded him. "Isn't that awful? They were hacked to pieces. They weren't even identifiable—the women ripped off all their clothes."

Ted stood beside his son, rubbing his hands.

"Here's what I think," Mark told him. "I think that proves they were really savages."

"All Indians?" Ted asked.

"Yes," Mark said. He said it with the kind of cockiness he had in those days, far too sure of himself. "Maybe not today anymore, but when the white people came to this land, some of those tribes were really Stone Age, Dad. I'm not kidding."

"What do you mean, *savages?*"

"The women and children chopped off their heads—that's what I'm telling you."

Mark claims his father went almost into a trance as he looked out over the battlefield and tried to imagine what might have happened—a swarm of women and children hacking away at bloodied bodies, the gentle sloping landscape unfurling violence, Indian women shaking limp legs from gray wool pants, flashing long knives over hair soaked in blood.

And then something happened, something so scary that Mark never forgot it. He seemed to lose his father. Poised there at the very spot of Custer's Last Stand, his father seemed to disappear from his body to a place he had tried so hard not to remember.

No one can know exactly what Ted saw in his mind just then, but we've all seen enough of the old pictures to know that the scorching images he must have seen right then—not the pictures but the real thing—were enough to take him right off the prairie and put him back in the middle of Europe.

Walls formed on an endless prairie vista, and soft grass melted into a thick and slimy morass, the stench of mud and excrement. The sky likely closed over Ted as if someone had drawn a final curtain, and he heard the sounds of Babel. Naked men, with thighs no thicker than a sapling birch. Eyes that seemed gouged. Hairless, sexless prisoners who stared at the GIs as if they were aliens. A man offered him a cigarette that he took because he felt obliged to honor the only gift the prisoner could offer. Many were crying, not in joy but in disbelief that whatever hell they'd been in was gone now with liberation.

Babel. Confusion of tongues. Whole rotting barracks full of men cowering in excrement and mud, grieving, it seemed, at death's having abandoned them. Madness. Anger. Screams. His men carried the dying outside into the sun, some of them screaming as if to have to live were horror.

First Lieutenant Ted Bennink watched all of that in his memory. What they'd found in the camp at Dachau—he hadn't expected it, hadn't expected anything close to what they'd found. How could anyone expect it? It was beyond imagination. What words can describe it?

To stare in those faces, to walk in that filth, to find stacks of bodies shoulder-high. "Christ," he'd said quietly, time and time again. "Jesus, my Lord," he'd said, to hold back—what? Tears? A pit of flesh and bones, torn rags. What language can be borrowed? Gray faces, the screams, Babel. Skin dried like mud falling from cheeks, thin and pasty. For a moment Ted was gone in a nightmare Mark didn't know.

"It's awful, Dad," he told his father. "Don't you think? It's just horrible what they did. And they were *women*."

"What's that?" Ted asked him, suddenly coming back.

"What they did—wasn't it awful?" Mark said.

164

We've all seen the pictures. Death spilling from freight cars standing closed and locked. You look, and you can't, and you *must*—but you can't lift your eyes for fear that if you do, you won't ever open them again. Twisted uniforms between layers of bodies scratched and mobbed on railroad cars that some German dog had never opened. "Jesus Christ my Lord," not even a prayer really—a chant, a benediction. Ted Bennink was there, one of the first.

"I mean, so it was their land, all right?" Mark told him. "None of them had deeds or anything, but it was all Indian land. That's true." He stopped and kicked at the ground. "But it's like they weren't even *human*, Dad. It was squaws that did it."

"Jesus," Ted said, and Mark looked at him strangely.

You couldn't look at any one of those prisoners with so many suffering, so many already dead. You couldn't look, but you couldn't turn your head.

Mark took hold of his father's arm. "Dad," he said.

And then he did the strangest thing, Mark says. Ted Bennink read words from his memory, chanted them as if out of nowhere. "I believe in God the Father, Almighty, Maker of heaven and earth." He pressed his lips together firmly, pulled his shoulders back, and raised his head. "And in Jesus Christ, His only begotten Son, our Lord."

Mark took his father's arm in both hands. "Dad," he said. "What is it? You okay?"

Ted looked directly at his son, angrily.

"What are you thinking about, Dad?" Mark said. "I don't get it."

Ted stumbled slowly back to Little Bighorn. "The squaws cut up the bodies, Mark?" Ted asked. "Is that what you're telling me?"

Mark put his arm around his father, kept a hand on his shoulder.

"Savages," Ted said, "it was something about savages?"

Then Mark took his arm back, afraid. "Maybe I'm wrong," he said.

Ted looked deeply into his son's eyes, as deep as he ever had, as if this were an admonition. "You want to say we had a right to kill them, Mark?" Ted asked. "Is that it?"

His son looked at him strangely. "Let's go," Mark told his father, and he walked around to the driver's side of the car. "You okay, Dad?" he asked again.

Ted Bennink, First Lieutenant Ted Bennink, had long ago stood by and watched as freed prisoners from the camp at Dachau—prisoners with frenzied Babel voices, prisoners still able to stand and breathe, who had lived on hate and revenge— killed, then mutilated what German guards they could catch. First Lieutenant Ted Bennink's own men—battle-toughened GIs from cities like Des Moines and small towns like Barneveld—machine-gunned unarmed SS butchers while the commanding officer, a quiet man from a small town in Iowa, stood dumb before them, the name Jesus coursing through his mind like a mantra.

"What I was saying about the squaws, Dad," Mark said, "you can't really prove anything by it, can you?"

The face of a German looked up from a twisted body slumped on the ground, a man who had been kicked mercilessly—a bald man, his face gone, empty and pallid, one arm up over his chest as he leaned on one elbow. He knew just enough of the old Dutch language of his grandfather—that's all Ted Bennink needed to understand the derision of the prisoners standing over the German, poised to kill him. "King of the Jews!" the shoeless prisoner screamed. "King of the Jews!" Then the prisoner spat on him, the man's whole face white. Already he was facing God. "King of the Jews!"

"Was it about getting shot, Dad?" Mark said. "Is that what you were thinking about?"

And then Ted looked at his son, who'd read so much, and

he smiled, the trance broken. "We're proud of you, Mark," Ted told him. He took the boy's arm. "Your mother and I are so proud of you."

The road at Little Bighorn winds through long slopes of open grass swaying in the wind, here and there are posted signs you can't read from the road, little monuments. Nothing else was said until once again the Black Hills rose from the horizon east.

But Mark never forgot that day he seemed to lose his father. Like Mary, the mother of Jesus, Mark had a way, even at sixteen, of pondering things in his heart.

It was Mark, a professor of history, who discovered what actually had happened fifty years before in southern Germany. He'd found a letter in a box of things his mother had given him to sift through after the funeral, a letter from a man in Pennsylvania who had written his father in 1946 to tell him that what the army had done to First Lieutenant Ted Bennink was injustice. It was wrong, the man said, since no one who wasn't there could know what they had seen at Dachau in April 1945. No one could understand.

Frantically, Mark searched for more information—something from the Pentagon maybe, some document, a letter, some record of what had happened or should have happened—something, anything.

Mark Bennink, the professor, knows how to research, and what he found was that his father, 45th Division, 147th Infantry, had been relieved of his command. What he discovered was that his father, the shoe repairman with the big beard, had stood by and watched chaos rule in the camp as Germans were maimed and murdered by some of his own men. That's what Mark discovered, only six weeks after his father's death.

Picture the professor there for a moment. He was at his desk overlooking a campus in the middle of the city. Books surrounded him on all sides, two of them his. He remembered high school history class, a paper he did on the Holocaust. He remembered bringing it home with an A, his father's silent approval, a gentle nod of pride. In all that time, the Ted Bennink who was not a lieutenant never spoke of what he had seen or done—or what he had not done.

Picture Mark there in his office, Mark the historian, looking out of his windows, the unfolded letter from an archives in Georgia bunched up on his desk, a letter full of history that came to the historian, so startlingly, as personal news.

His only thought was of failure—not his father's at the camp in Germany, but his own in not learning history from the man who made it, in not letting his father breathe the truth about his own life.

It's February, warm for winter, and right then and there Professor Mark Bennink canceled his classes in order to go home to Barneveld.

"What did I know about him and the war?" his mother said. She looked closely at her son. Her grandson, eating Cheerios from a small plastic cup, one by one, sat on her lap. "Very, very little." And she told Mark this story.

"One Fourth of July when you were just a baby—that's how I remember it, Mark—you were just a baby and you cried and cried and cried. But we couldn't leave the park because your brother wouldn't hear of it. Art was already ten, and he loved all the fireworks.

"We'd put down the blanket. Marie was just a child and she sat in Ted's arm the whole time, not crying, but scared to death almost, I remember, sitting there between her father's legs.

"Mark, you couldn't have been two—you were maybe fifteen months, just walking, and every one of those rockets, you know—what do you call those things? Every one of them would make this big thump when it went up, and I'd try to close myself around you because you were so scared.

"We were out on the football field, and the mosquitoes

were thick in the grass—my goodness, the welts you used to carry. Does he swell up like you did?" She pointed at Josh, the little boy.

Mark nodded. "Yeah, he does."

"Poor thing. Anyhow, it never once dawned on me that it might be hard on your father—all those explosions. Of course, there I was with my arms full of a crying child and nowhere to go, Art just having the time of his life. Oh, Mark, there's a time in a mother's life when it's all you can do is think of the kids, and I wasn't thinking of your father at all.

"You need a drink, honey?" She leaned over and kissed her youngest grandchild. "What a thing to do, Mark, having a baby at your age—and Marcia's. My word. What a thing to do."

"Did he say something that night?" Mark said.

"When it was finally over, we went home and he put Art to bed. Your brother, Art, wasn't his son, Mark, you have to remember that. Why don't you get me a tissue over there? Can you reach that box by the cookie jar? Thanks.

"Art was higher than a kite, going all over the house like something lit up himself—you know, 'boom, boom, boom!' Marie wanted the light on in the bedroom, and meanwhile I had to carry you all over because you were still scared stiff. Can you imagine that, Mark—me carrying you all over? But you would not be put down.

"It had to be midnight by the time it was all quiet in the house, and just the two of us up. Both of us were really tired, I remember. We went to the porch—you know, that was before air conditioning, and you know how hot it is here every Fourth.

"Oh, I had a wonderful husband, Mark. Sometimes I watch *Oprah* and I think I'm something really strange because I never once didn't love him. Everybody's got their faults and of course we had quarrels too—but, my goodness, I miss him, Mark. Somebody my age—you'd wonder what's an old woman miss in a man? But I miss him every hour of the day—believe me."

"What'd he say, Mom?"

"I said to him, just as innocent, I said, 'Honey, you're tired, aren't you? It's been quite a day.'

"And he looks at me, and he says something like this—I don't remember it exactly. He says, 'It's hard to believe sometimes how good life can be.'

"Well, I hugged him, Mark, because I thought it was your dad's way of saying that all of this—scrambling kids and bawling babies—was worth it. I thought he was saying he loved me. I did. So I hugged him, see?

"And he didn't say much, but I could tell that what I was thinking he had meant was only part of the truth. It was like he stayed cold in my arms. So I said to him—this is just what I said or something like it—'Are you happy?' Not that I doubted it either. I suppose I said it for myself, because I was. Even though it was hard—him just starting the shoe business and all, and sometimes he had pain with his wounds. But I was happy, Mark, I *was*—even though during the war there were times—like when Chuck was killed—that I thought nothing would ever be good again ever for me in life.

"And then he says to me, he says, 'Katharine, I want you to know just one thing: In this life, I've already been to hell.'

"I still had my arms around him, and I didn't move. It was so unlike your father to use a word like that because he was—and you know this too—always so close to God, it seemed. So I knew right away that he was talking about the war, and I never even thought of pushing him any farther because I thought then that if there was something he thought I should know, he would tell me—if not that Fourth of July, then some other night when it was just the two of us out on the front porch alone again and he wanted to speak."

"That's it?" Mark said.

Katharine pinched her grandson's face with her fingers. "Oh, Mark," she said, "I just don't know what to say about this little blessing of yours. What a dear! Just sits so happy here. What a good child."

"That's all you know, Mom?" Mark said.

"If he wanted me to know, I thought he'd tell me. But he never did, and I never asked. And soon enough I didn't care about not knowing. But your father was not a man at war, Mark—you know that too. I'll tell you what happened," she said. "You saw the scars on his behind. You must have seen them, Mark."

"Sure I saw them," he said.

"They healed—that's what happened." She raised her face, her chin, with a kind of arrogance that Mark had never really seen before. "Mark," she said, "I lost a husband at the beginning of that war, and I almost lost another right at the end."

Even Mark the historian had almost forgotten that his mother had already buried two husbands.

After breakfast and morning coffee the next day, Professor Mark Bennink, his wife, and their little caboose, Joshua Theodore, left for Des Moines. Mark left without telling his mother anything of what he'd discovered about her husband.

Today, Barneveld people have to remind themselves that Mark Bennink is a professor of history at Drake University, a man who has written books on Iowa history. Not many Barneveld kids grow up to write books, but then very few Barneveld people read them either. The local library has both of Mark's books— three copies of each, no waiting.

But hundreds of people in town won't forget the three-point play that Mark made in the waning seconds of the district play-offs his senior year. He was fouled on a pump fake, and the shot went in. Barneveld beat Algona, a much bigger school.

So when Mark's name came up as a possible speaker at the Memorial Day doings at the park downtown, the committee remembered him as one of the town's premiere athletes, and they reminded themselves that he was also a professor of history, and therefore a fine and fitting candidate.

So Mark stood downtown this May, across from his father's store, the howitzer there beside him in the kind of soaking rain the proverb promises in April. He was the only professional historian in the crowd of more than four hundred people, mostly old folks, the only one who knew that the World War II commemorative plaque that has stood in that park now for forty-some years is plain wrong: His father, wounded twice in street fighting in the final days of the European campaign, was no first lieutenant when the war ended. That's a lie.

For a time at least, I know a battle raged in Mark's mind, because he knew what had really happened and he thought the whole story would make the greatest Memorial Day speech possible—the immense price of freedom, the necessity of horrifying memories. But his father's silence won that battle. Professor Mark honored Ted Bennink's memory with a conventional homily on vigilance and courage, and he never told Barneveld his father's story. Katharine was there, of course, with an entourage of widows, all of whom said what a fine speech it was, how fitting, and, of course, how proud Katharine must be of such a smart son.

But with all of his research skills, with all of his academic connections, with all of the accumulated wisdom from his own broad and in-depth understanding of history and the human condition, Professor Mark Bennink could not understand how his father, who was among the first in the gate at Dachau, could live so peacefully, even joyfully, in the world of Barneveld—or anywhere, for that matter—after what he'd seen and not done. Even Mark didn't understand his father's peace.

Ted told me in the last days he was alive how he had been able to find peace.

July 2, 1952. Two days before the ten o'clock fireworks in

Barneveld. It was six in the morning, and Ted Bennink had put on the coffee downstairs. Katharine was still in bed, as were the children.

Ted was reading from a devotional booklet written by a preacher in Indiana and published by his own church press, a booklet of meditations that happened to be, that month, on the Apostles' Creed, a devotional that preacher likely intended to bring healing, but would have never imagined doing so successfully. That morning, Ted Bennink ran into some thoughts on the single line "he descended into hell."

"Maybe none of us knows for sure what hell is," that preacher wrote, "but we know for certain that it is, at least, the worst we can ever imagine."

Ted looked up from the booklet, heard the percolator bumping up fresh coffee on the stove, and watched a blue jay flutter down from the linden tree outside his window to chase a sparrow off the feeder Katharine had hung from the clothesline pole.

If there was anything he was sure of, it was that he'd once seen hell.

"The blessing of Christian love is that Christ was there," that preacher wrote. "He suffered too—the very worst of our pain—so that we might live. Jesus Christ descended into hell."

Ted Bennink shut the booklet without even reading the prayer at the bottom of the page. He fixed in his mind the only image of Jesus he knew—that serene face, the long hair, the glow as he sits, hands folded on a rock at Gethsemane, pleading with the Father. He turned the pages of an album of despair and death at Dachau, scanned the empty, hollow faces that he'd seen, skulls in layer after layer peering out from the barracks at the camp.

Which one was Jesus? he asked himself.

The few still breathing from the death train, drawn painfully from the stack of corpses, a tangle of arms and legs.

He was there, Ted Bennink told himself.

The bald German, ready to die, his legs split, knees splayed, his body crooked on the ground, an arm up as if to protect his already torn face. He knew better than to beg anyone for mercy. "King of the Jews," the inmate had said, mockingly.

And himself. First Lieutenant Ted Bennink. His helmet set back on his head, the rifle at his side. All the time repeating the name of Jesus—Jesus my Lord, Jesus my Lord—as if the words wouldn't be stanched.

Someplace Jesus Christ was there in hell.

He descended into hell.

Christ knew everything. He was there, Ted thought. He felt every last thing. He was there. He descended into hell.

My God, Ted thought, my Savior and my King. He knows what happened. My Lord God knows. No one else may ever understand. But Jesus Christ my Savior was there.

It may shock you to think that the shoe salesman Ted Bennink allowed the massacre he did in the camp at Dachau, the avenging murder of Nazi guards. You may side with the army on this one. You may think it wrong that he lost control.

But as Ted would say, you weren't there.

And on that July morning and for the rest of his life, all that mattered to Ted Bennink was that his Lord was there. Jesus his Savior *knew*.

This is the story of Ted Bennink's peace, a story he didn't want told, not because of his guilt, but because of the darkness and horror of events he never wanted to relive or others even to know. The memories were there, always, but one July morning, peace came into his heart and stayed there for all those years in the shoe shop downtown, right across from the memorial howitzer—peace that stuck to his soul like that old countertop buffalo nickel.

Mins
the Scavenger

Mins De Boom spent thirty-seven years of his life in school but never received a formal education. No one, not even his mother, ever thought of him as smart. For thirty years he worked in the town of Barneveld as the school janitor. He spent only seven years as a student himself, and those years passed long ago when he was a boy in the country of his birth, the Netherlands, before the war and before he immigrated.

In the small Dutch town where he lived, his mother died on a Saturday afternoon in 1947 while she sat smiling and seemingly contented in her rocking chair, having just concluded her housecleaning, something she did always with religious devotion. Her house in order, she'd sat down, people said, prepared as she was at that very moment of every week for death or the Sabbath, whichever came first.

That was two years after the war and four years after Mins's father had been deported to Germany by Nazis, never to return. With his mother gone and the country in shambles, what was left for Mins, he thought, but immigration? Long before the war, distant family had immigrated to a place called "Iowa." Often, he'd tried to draw his lips into the position it took to pronounce such a strange word.

When he arrived in New York, he called his Uncle John in Barneveld. "John," he said, "I'm here. Come and get me." He didn't imagine America to be such a huge place.

His Uncle John found Mins that job as a janitor in the Barneveld school, where he would arrive each day before the students, look over the list of tasks he'd written up for himself the day before, and start in on washrooms, doormats, and windows, forever full of smudges from children's dirty hands. Once classes began, he loved the silence in the empty corridors, the attentive humming behind every closed door, children busy learning. At the end of the day, with the blackboards clean and hallways shining, Mins assessed his little corner of God's creation and pronounced it very good.

He had only one vice to speak of, an old-world custom he never lost: He smoked cigarettes—fat, lumpy things he rolled himself, a habit the school board tried to discourage him from practicing in school. But on cold days, when he couldn't sneak out back of the school's machine shop, he would sit in the boiler room once classes had begun and have his first smoke. It wasn't much of a vice, really.

Sometimes the high school boys kidded him. "Hey, Mins," they'd say, "how about you roll us a joint?" But he would simply squint and smile and shrug his shoulders. "I only been here yet thirty years," he'd say. "I don't know the language so good."

He came from a place in Holland where even the Dutch consider folks to be narrow and backward; and when Mins's only relative in the States, Uncle John, passed on, he never had an opportunity to grow. He despised television and loved the church. Perhaps *love* isn't the right word. Worship, to Mins, was something as essential as cleaning.

The truth is Mins was loved as a janitor, and when he retired, the school board gave him a gold watch he wore only on Sunday. He treasured that watch more than anything he had ever been given in life—other than his wife, that is, whose feelings hadn't always been reciprocal.

It may surprise you to hear that such a simple man as Mins would find a wife, but he married Lena Mars because he thought her children needed a father—and, after all, he was alone and therefore eligible. She consented, or so people say, for something of the same reason. Besides, with her ex-husband's dismal record of child support, living with Mins was preferable, in Barneveld especially, to the public dole.

Her former husband had left with another woman, and while everyone in the little church where both of them worshiped felt that what the man had done was an abomination, most of them secretly felt his actions understandable, given Lena's shrill tongue and deep moodiness—gifts, people said, she came by honestly, if you knew her parents.

I married them in the strangest marriage ceremony at which I ever had the privilege of officiating—in the living room of Mins's little home across from the cemetery, no more than four or five people in attendance, and very little show of love. Their marriage was a matter of convenience, a case of two single people deciding to put away their loneliness.

No one in town knew much about the marriage of Mins and Lena, and although no one can really know for sure what happens in any bedroom save his or her own, such a fact didn't keep people from speculating. They guessed the marriage was consummated several times that first year, maybe occasionally the next, and almost certainly never thereafter, when, nightly, the neighbors began to see the lights in two bedrooms turned out almost simultaneously.

Mins De Boom was no ordinary man. He had not married Lena Mars out of all-consuming passion, nor even from some desire to heal his loneliness, a stranger, as he was, in a strange land. Psychologists might claim Mins himself had no sense of his own motivations, that what he really wanted was less philanthropic at bottom, let us say, than libidinal. But those psychologists need also to consider Lena carefully—a woman most men would say lit no libidinal fires herself.

Quite frankly, Mins De Boom made an unusual American

177

because he expected so little from life. Perhaps it was his old country background, or his lack of education; perhaps it was the war, when he'd spent weeks looking for food out in the country surrounding the little Dutch village. Perhaps it was the time he'd spent hidden away in the storage space he built himself to hide from the German roundups that had already taken his father. Then again, perhaps it was his faith, which taught him that storing up treasures in huge barns would only get him rather unceremoniously stuck in the eye of a sewing needle.

When he married Lena, Mins likely never demanded the kind of intimacy commonly thought normal by the standards of American television, standards he knew nothing of. He was already fifty years old—as was she, nearly—and he harbored no dreams of procreation.

What's more, in the home in which he'd grown up, displays of affection were thought gypsy-ish, the mark of someone, well, unsteady. Once the Germans took his father away forever, he had no patterns for marital love.

I visited with Mins often, and I know he was a man happy with very little of what the world thinks absolutely necessary. And he and Lena, after the kind of initial tribulation expected of any newlyweds—maybe a bit more—began to appreciate each other, although quietly, for their mutual sturdiness.

When Mins retired, he didn't simply excuse himself from living, as some do. He decided to walk the country ditches and clean the highways of trash, scavenging for bottles and cans thrown there in large part by students whose refuse he'd been retrieving for years already. After all those years inside, he wanted to be in the beautiful sunshine. Besides, each can was worth a nickel.

You should have seen him. He had an old bicycle, the kind popular twenty years ago—thick tires, a seat as wide as a tractor's, and a wire-mesh basket leaning over the front handlebars, a style quite popular in the Netherlands. Over the back fender he'd affixed an additional pair of baskets, and he sewed for himself a very wide and deep nylon duffel bag he could throw over his shoulders like a knapsack. Lena bought him a straw hat at a garage sale, a Panama with a single white band, which he wore to keep the sun off his bald head. On hot days he wore one of several old mesh football jerseys he'd redeemed from the school trash—but never shorts. What would people say, anyway, in Holland, about a man who ran around with such crooked legs all bare?

He kept a weekly route—Monday, north to Perkins, both sides of the road; Tuesday, south to Million Dollar Corner; Wednesday, east to the county line; and Thursday, west along the blacktop to Middleburg. On Fridays he hit the gravel roads right around town, and on Saturday he stayed home with Lena to clean house. Sundays, of course, he went to church.

He became a suntanned scavenger, cleaning the roadside of the refuse people throw unthinkingly from cars and trucks. What he found in those ditches often made him more sure that one of the doctrines of the faith with which he was reared was accurate to the human condition—original sin. Of course, he didn't say it quite that way. He often shook his head at what he found and wondered how people could be so much like pigs.

One Tuesday, on a hot afternoon south of town where the West Branch Creek elbows across the highway, Mins De Boom was walking through the ditch grass when he came upon a case—black, square, and of significant size. He had found things before that were valuable—a good jacket, a pair of boots, once or twice a wallet he'd returned forthwith, and enough T-shirts to fill a closet. But this was something unusual. The scuff marks on its corners were an indication that it may have been thrown, like everything else, from a passing car.

He picked it up and ran his fingers along the leather, smudging out dirt marks. Then he dropped the bag of cans in the grass and looked up at the road to see if anyone had seen him

179

pick up what he'd discovered. When he saw no cars, he raised his knee and tried to open the case, but it was too big to open against his leg. He sat down and laid the case in front of him. There was no lock, only a pair of clasps that opened easily. When he raised the top, he was amazed to find, inside, a viola.

Now you might wonder how it is that a man like Mins De Boom even recognized this instrument as a viola—after all, most people in Barneveld wouldn't know a viola from a bass viol. The truth is Mins's mother had played the viola in the old country. She played it often after her husband had been taken away in those dark days of the war, on the nights when it was quiet and Mins and Lexie, the little Jewish girl they'd hid for a time, sat in the kitchen and waited out the occupation.

This viola was more orange in color than the one he remembered his mother playing, but it was a viola nonetheless, tucked perfectly in red felt. Two bows were clasped within the top of the case, along with a half-dozen extra strings in square paper bags. There was resin in the little compartment in the bottom, plus a strap of some type to wear over the shoulder.

Mins looked up once more and thought about his bicycle, a quarter-mile on the other side of the bridge, lying far enough down into the ditch not to be noticed by passersby. The roar of cattle trucks on the highway not fifty feet away from his head nearly suffocated his daring, but once they had passed, he took out the viola and held it in his hands—warm, it seemed, with life. It must have been lying in the sun since dawn.

It was, as are all great handcrafted instruments, something of a miracle—light and shiny, the chevrons of wood grain down its back almost translucent as Mins spun the instrument slowly in his hands. The ebony chin rest was scuffed with wear, like the fingerboard.

Inside the compartment with the resin, he'd seen a silver tuning fork, not unlike his mother's. With the neck of the viola in one hand, the bottom resting on his knee, he picked up the tuning fork and hit it lightly against the edge of the case, creating a tone so clear he thought it might have come from God.

He put down the fork and lifted the viola to his chin, curled his fingers around the neck, and plucked the last string, the A-string. Then he reached up to the scroll and turned the peg slightly to measure the sound against the tone still singing in his ear.

Holding the viola in place, he closed the case once more with his right hand, then noted that the sun had not yet bleached the leather. It must have been there for no more than a day, at most, he thought.

It was, I think, the sheer pleasure of holding the instrument in his hands that made him feel suddenly guilty. He took hold of the handle of the case, held the viola in his right hand, then slid himself even deeper into the ditch to avoid being seen by the cars and trucks passing above him on Highway 75.

He reopened the case and laid the instrument down once more. Then he removed the top bow from its clasps, tightened the horsehair slightly, as his mother had always done, retrieved the viola in his left hand, lifted it again to his chin, turned his neck to make its position comfortable, and slowly ran the bow over the A-string. So many years had passed since he'd heard the throaty sound of even the instrument's highest string that he was surprised to feel within himself some strange urgency he could identify only with those dark nights of the occupation, Lexie's dark eyes doleful, needing so much hope.

By this time, you may have guessed what was to happen at that spot, deep in the ditch beside Highway 75. It is, of course, the miracle of this story, something of a miracle of life.

Mins De Boom sat in the ditch and played that viola, even though he had never had a lesson. Who knows what kind of holy passion it was that occupied his instinct to enable his fingers to locate the proper distances over the fingerboard? Was it a memory of his mother's playing in the shadowed candlelight years ago? Was it something left unopened for almost fifty years?

He sat with his knees up against the slope and played an old psalm that came back to him as if it were perched forever in his memory. He played that psalm in his mother's old way, in a way she'd played such pieces for Lexie, a way she thought Davidic, slow and relentless, each note something to be treasured and marked and encased in a glass box, the whole stanza a kind of museum.

A lesser man would have cried, perhaps, to discover, after so many years, such a gift in his fingers. A lesser man would have wept simply to remember those moments he had tried to lock away in his memory. But whatever quaking Mins De Boom may have felt within his soul or his heart was not shown so much on his face as it was felt in the tremor of the notes that rose from the strings of a viola someone had carelessly dropped in the ditch of Highway 75.

From the moment Mins De Boom put down the instrument that morning, he knew he could never again part with it, no matter what the circumstances. He brought it slowly to his knee and laid it carefully back in the case, then fixed the bow into the clasps at the top, snapped the button on the resin compartment, and laid the solitary piece of red felt cloth down perfectly over the bridge and strings, just as he'd found it. Then he closed the case securely and held it over his chest, as if there were no handle.

Country ditches today are full of plastic. Large sheets of black plastic rip away from the silage covers on farms all over this county and blow in the stiff prairie winds, then catch on barbed wire, where they hang like black flags until the wind itself shreds them into pieces that eventually blow away forever.

Mins found a broad shard of black plastic and wound the case inside, then carried it under his arm in the bottom of the ditch, all the way to the bridge, where his bicycle lay. He knew that some of the passersby might recognize that he'd found something unusual, since on ordinary days the twin baskets

over the back tire of his bicycle were filled with cans and bottles, so he lowered the viola carefully into one of those rear
baskets after dumping the cans he'd picked up earlier into the
basket on the other side. Forgetting the rest of the ditch for
that day, he pedaled back into town.

Some people remember seeing him that morning, not
because of the black bundle in his basket, but because of the
way he kept his face down beneath the brim of that Panama
straw hat Lena had bought him, not as if he were fighting a
terrifying northwest wind or driving rain, but as if he wanted
no one to recognize his triumphal entry.

If there's one thing Mins is not, it's invisible. After all those
years as the school janitor, he knew most of the people in
town—and most knew him. But then, perhaps no one human
being ever really knows another. Who at Barneveld Calvary
would have guessed that Mins De Boom could play the viola?

When he came home, he unwrapped the case from the black
plastic and stood it in the garage. Lena was out hanging clothes.
She came in when it was standing there, unwrapped, on the
work bench. For her, he drew the viola carefully from the case
and showed it to her, holding it in two hands, as if it were an
offering.

"Whose is it?" she asked.

He told her where he'd found it.

"It must be worth something," she told him. "You should
advertise."

Mins nodded, but, as you might expect, he didn't intend to.

The next day Lena came out to the garage and saw it there
yet, and she reminded Mins that it would only be right to try
to get it back to its owner. She told him he could call in to
"Swap Shop," the local radio show. "There may be a reward,"
she told him. "Besides," she said, "if no one answers the ad,
we can sell it ourselves."

Mins knew all of that to be true.

183

I wish I knew why he didn't play that viola for Lena, right then and there. He may have guessed it would shock her to know he could play the way he could. Maybe he feared the fragile balance of their relationship would be threatened by her knowing his secret. On the other hand, maybe the memory was so deeply secured within him that it couldn't emerge in the presence of another human being in this foreign country.

I never heard him play it myself, but he told me he found it, and he told me that music came from it magically as he played it in the grass at the side of the highway.

Three days later, when they drove the car into the garage after church on a Sunday morning, she saw the viola standing there still. "Surely you don't mean to keep it?" she asked him. "It must be valuable."

"Oh, no—no, no, no," Mins told her. "This week I will for sure put an ad in the *Shopper*."

Now the whole town knew that if something was lost in the ditches outside of town, Mins De Boom would have seen it. Perhaps he himself might have found it. And once the Straaks family determined that their daughter's viola had inadvertently fallen from their van one night, Mr. Straaks called Mins De Boom.

"Mins," he said, his voice booming over the phone, "my daughter somehow lost her viola. We think maybe it went in the ditch up from Million Dollar Corner."

Mins's ears burned.

"You didn't spot it, did you?"

Mins heard his wife pick up another phone in the basement.

"It had to be the only lost viola in the ditch south of town," Mr. Straaks joked.

Mins, being Mins, had no choice—not only because Lena was listening. The simple scavenger couldn't lie deftly; in fact, about such things he couldn't lie at all.

"You should see my daughter," Mr. Straaks said. "She's absolutely heartbroken. Not to mention the fact that it wasn't exactly cheap."

"This viola," he asked, "it's orange colored?"

"Yes," Mr. Straaks said. "Yes, of course, that's the one. I'm sure."

"It's here, in my garage."

"Oh, thank God," Mr. Straaks said. "Listen, I can't get over there anymore tonight, but first thing in the morning, all right? First thing in the morning, I'll send my daughter over— she'll be so relieved."

Lena never said a word. To her, the viola was a lucky find. She hoped that the Straaks, whom she knew because of the tall pillars on their beautiful new home across town, would give them a generous reward.

That night, late, when Lena was already asleep, Mins got a strange notion into his mind, something that got him up and out of his bed and made him leave the bedroom across from hers. It was, of course, the viola. He lit a candle he kept on the workbench in the garage and lifted the instrument out of its case with the same care he had that first morning he'd found it. Then he looked back at the door to the house. He undid a bow, and waited there like a soloist for a nod from the maestro, the neck of the instrument in his left hand. He walked back to the door and opened it, listened for any noise at all. By the light of the candle, he could see the time on the old classroom clock he'd hung above the workbench. It was after two.

What he must have felt was the naked desire to have that delicate instrument make its music, for he didn't think of what he'd felt that morning in the ditch as *his* playing really— never considered that what beauty emerged from that viola had, in fact, been prompted by anything within his janitor's soul. The music was to him, as so much was, simply some-

185

thing as divine as sunshine, something it was even a bit of sin to deny once more. He looked around him at the faint shadows dancing off the slate walls of the garage, but determined the garage was not the place for the music that he knew would come again.

He was afraid to start the car, afraid to raise the mechanical garage door he had recently installed, so he had no choice. He had to steal away quietly, carrying the instrument, so he left the garage out the front door, hiding the viola beneath his bathrobe as he walked down the driveway to the street and toward the place that seemed suddenly God-sent—the Barneveld cemetery.

When he saw the dampness shine on the grass in the moon's bright glow, he took off his slippers as if he were back at home in his mother's house. He walked barefoot far to the back of the graveyard, to the place where the town, years ago, had begun burying the children who'd died unexpectedly. It was a spot not that far from the school where he'd worked for so many years, quite a distance from any house in the neighborhood.

Marv Bleeker is a cop in town. Part of his ritual is checking doors on Main Street businesses and sometimes churches. That night, he parked the squad car on the downtown side of Calvary Church, and he walked around the whole building, rattling knobs. Over on the east side, he said, he suddenly heard something that sounded almost unearthly. It was 2:46, he says, because he looked at his watch to verify what he heard was no dream.

You see, Mins De Boom played that viola once more, the last time he would ever touch that instrument—or any like it—in his lifetime. In the cemetery, he wrapped his clean fingers gently around the neck and brought the bow softly to the strings again, calling up music his mother had played so many years before, music he'd heard sometimes when hidden away in that storage space while waiting for the Nazis to climb back into their vehicles, his entire repertoire those very same hymns and psalms.

Across the street and up the block, a huge mercury-vapor lamp stands over the parking lot at Calvary Church. Bleeker said he stole out across the street onto the grass of the cemetery, and there he spotted Mins. From that point, he said, sitting there looking over the forest of graves, he almost forgot for a moment that the glints and shimmering echoes on the stones of the cemetery really came from that strong light up the hill and behind him, that lamp affixed to the wall of the church, catty-corner from the west edge of the cemetery.

I like to believe that if I had seen Mins with that viola, barefoot and in his bathrobe, and if I had listened to his music, playing something in his soul I'm not sure even he understood, I might have seen the same vision Bleeker did in the light playing off the shiny granite monuments. Those flashes seemed like the eyes of decades of school children, all of them sitting respectfully for a guest concert by a renowned musician, an accomplished European master, playing for God and, then again, himself. That's what Bleeker told me.

The next day, little Sylvia Straaks came by happily to retrieve her viola. Mins stood with a stubborn smile and handed it to her, noting especially the joy and relief on the child's face.

Only Marv Bleeker heard Mins De Boom play the viola that somehow had come to him as a gift, albeit for such a short time. Mins died last month, a complication of the cancer he suffered from. Perhaps, as the school board said, he should have stopped rolling his own cigarettes. It will comfort you to know that Lena attended him faithfully through those hours when he quite gingerly, in fact, approached his death—having years before already approached his Lord with steady hands.

187

Now you may think I've merely made all of this up, this story of my good friend Mins the musician. But your skeptical minds will have to be satisfied with the truth as I've told it here in this story of long silences and just a few songs.

As Mins himself might have said, "Those who have ears will listen."

Epilogue

Not long ago, I sat in a group of eight pastors. We were attending a convention of preachers, a stadium full of thousands of them. After the usual spirited preaching up on the platform, we broke into small groups for discussion and prayer. What I experienced there was deep hurt among those men of God—broken marriages, broken spirits, broken promises. Disillusionment threatened many of them—not disillusionment with God, although some of that was confessed as well—but disillusionment with their calling as spiritual leaders.

Disillusionment grows when the disparity widens between what we know we are and what we think we should be. Some Christians call worship *celebration* today, and with good reason—it is. But sometimes today Christianity becomes so synonymous with smiles that in many congregations it may be difficult to locate the meek, the poor in spirit, or those who mourn—all of them especially blessed by Jesus' own Beatitudes. We seem committed to the idea that on Sunday we best communicate God's love with bright shiny faces, and no one has to smile more broadly than a pastor, the man of God. Yet, as all will attest, no one knows better the real joys and concerns.

The stories I've told you are the unspoken joys and concerns of a church I've called Barneveld Calvary, stories told to me in a confidence so significant that the state recognizes the impropriety of stepping between myself, the preacher, and those whose stories I know from their own confessions.

No court of law can require me to reveal the secrets I've told you freely.

None of these stories were ever told—probably for good reasons. Not all of them soothe the soul; some of them fit rather awkwardly into our pretentious sense of the grand narrative of our lives. All are personal. They have nothing glitzy about them; they are not simply cute. They are, for better or for worse, our stories.

But if time is nothing more than a construct the eternal God gives us to manage our lives, then our stories, fashioned as they are in human time, are not our own. They belong to God. After all, only he knows how they'll end. It is, I believe, a fact of our existence that even though each of us keeps getting it wrong, God almighty keeps on listening and loving. He has written eternity.

The blessing of the gospel is not simply our happiness but eternal joy that tells so much more than a smiley face shows, joy that comes from two humbling realizations—that our sin is real, and that it is gone.

That's the whole story, the real good news.

An English professor at Dordt College, **James Calvin Schaap** is the author of many published short stories and the recently released *In the Silence There Are Ghosts: A Novel*. He has been awarded top prizes from the Evangelical Press Association for his writings, and he has twice won the Iowa Arts Council's annual award for fiction.